Murder at a Vineyard Mansion

Murder at a Vineyard Mansion

A Martha's Vineyard Mystery

Philip R. Craig

THORNDIKE
CHIVERS

This Large Print edition is published by Thorndike Press®,
Waterville, Maine USA and by BBC Audiobooks, Ltd,
Bath, England.

Published in 2004 in the U.S. by arrangement with Scribner,
an imprint of Simon & Schuster, Inc.

Published in 2004 in the U.K. by arrangement with the author.

U.S. Hardcover 0-7862-6625-2 (Mystery)
U.K. Hardcover 1-4056-3083-3 (Chivers Large Print)

The text of this Large Print edition is unabridged.
Other aspects of the book may vary from the original edition.

Set in 16 pt. Plantin by Elena Picard.

Printed in the United States on permanent paper.

British Library Cataloguing-in-Publication Data available

Library of Congress Cataloging-in-Publication Data

Craig, Philip R., 1933–
    Murder at a Vineyard mansion : a Martha's Vineyard
mystery / Philip R. Craig.
        p. cm.
    ISBN 0-7862-6625-2 (lg. print : hc : alk. paper)
    1. Jackson, Jeff (Fictitious character) — Fiction.
    2. Private investigators — Massachusetts — Fiction.
    3. Martha's Vineyard (Mass.) — Fiction. 4. Large type
books. I. Title.
PS3553.R23M87 2004b
    813'.54—dc22   2004047374

For the real police officers
on the real island of Martha's Vineyard,
who protect and serve
and stay human while doing it.

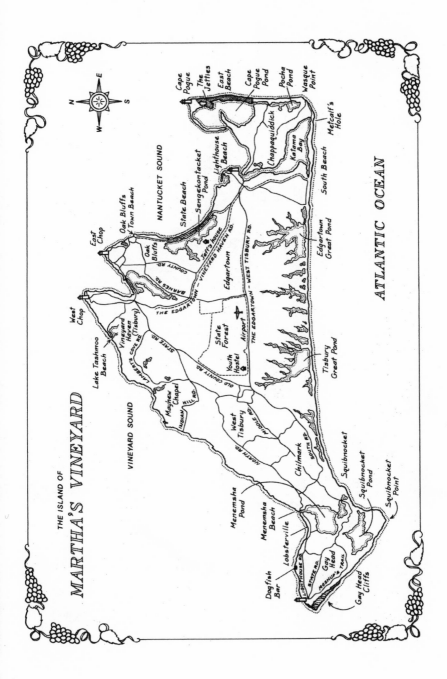

THE ISLAND OF
MARTHA'S VINEYARD

O Love, be fed with apples while you may,
And feel the sun and go in royal array . . .
A smiling innocent
Exquisite in the pulse of tainted blood . . .

— Robert Graves, "Sick Love"

1

I was coming out of the Dock Street Coffee Shop at the foot of Main Street when I saw Sergeant Tony D'Agostine of the Edgartown PD step out of his cruiser and head in my direction. He apparently needed a caffeine hit to keep him going for the rest of his shift.

"What's up on the mean streets?" I asked.

"Well," he said, "Mickey Gomes escaped from jail last night and hasn't come back."

The county jail in Edgartown looks more like a nice big white house than a jail, and Mickey wasn't the first person to break out of it. None of the escapees ever stay escaped very long, though, because Martha's Vineyard is an island so there's only so far you can run and the police know most of the places you can hide.

"What do you mean he hasn't come back?" I asked.

"I mean that he's escaped several times

9

in the last year, usually after supper. But he's always come back in time for breakfast. This time, though, a jailer noticed he was missing and our best guess is that when Mickey saw a bunch of cops wandering around the jail, he was afraid to come back so he went and hid."

"What's he in for?"

"Statutory rape. He got it on with a fifteen-year-old girl a couple of years ago. This escape isn't anything to worry about. He's not dangerous and we know where he is."

"Where's that?"

"Up in the woods by the girl's house. When he breaks out he spends the night with her. According to her parents, she's seven months pregnant with his child."

I did some fast calculating. "Sired on one of his jailbreaks, I take it."

"You take it right. She's seventeen now and he's twenty and they want to get hitched, but the honeymoon will have to wait until he does the extra time for breaking jail. He had bad luck getting nailed now because he only had a couple more weeks to serve. Mickey's not too bright, but then again he had no reason to think he'd get caught this time because he never got caught before."

10

"How come nobody noticed him escaping until now?"

"I hear two stories. First, that the prisoners complained about not having any privacy, so the jail keepers stopped checking up on them too closely; second, that the sheriff's wife ordered the surveillance cameras turned off so no one would catch her making whoopee with her favorite inmate. Anyway, just before they locked the cells for the night Mickey would put a fake head — I saw it and it's a pretty cheesy one if you ask me — on his pillow and then go down the hall to the john. Only instead of turning right and going into the toilet, he'd turn left and go out the window of a storage room. Somebody'd slipped him a screwdriver and he'd just take the screen off the window and leave. The next morning he'd come back and put the screen back on. All the prisoners knew about it, but none of the jail keepers did. He only got found out this time because a jailer happened to wander down the hall last night and find the storage room screen gone."

"And now all has been revealed."

"Some of it, anyway. Once the jail keepers found out he had escaped, the prisoners told them how he's been doing it for months. They thought it was pretty funny. I can see that you do, too."

"You'd better get yourself that coffee," I said. "You need to be wide-awake if you're going to bring in a hard case like Mickey Gomes."

"No problem," said Tony. "He'll be getting hungry about now, since he's missed breakfast. I don't think he'll hide very long."

"Keep me informed of the latest developments."

"Sure." Tony went into the coffee shop and I climbed into my old Land Cruiser and drove home. I'd forgotten to ask Tony how the Silencer case was going, but I figured that if they'd solved it he'd have told me.

Actually I thought there was a good chance that they'd never catch the Silencer because, in spite of his victims' outrage, looking for him probably got less police attention than any other case on the island. This was because the cops, like most of the other people on the Vineyard, including me, were much more sympathetic toward the criminal than his victims. The cops couldn't admit this, of course, but their efforts to apprehend him were pretty feeble at best.

For the Silencer had become a folk hero by doing one incredibly popular if totally illegal thing: he destroyed the sound systems in those cars that came boom-boom-booming down the island's roads and streets, always with the windows rolled down, always heard approaching a mile away, always throbbing with ground-shaking bass notes, always offending everyone but the driver and people just like him.

Why such drivers always have their windows down and the volume turned as high as it will go is a mystery to all who don't engage in such sound production, and what to do about it is a constant, infuriating frustration to everyone but the drivers. Or it had been until the coming of the Silencer, who that spring had begun destroying the sound systems of some of the loudest cars on the island. He hadn't gotten them all, but he had gotten several and he was still getting them.

The car owners were, of course, furious, not to say out of hundreds of dollars per car, and were quick to accuse the island cops of incompetence for failing to capture the person who had soon and for the most part affectionately become known as the Silencer.

Or perhaps it was now plural Silencers, for speculation had it that copycat criminals were beginning to operate, since not only automobile sound systems were being destroyed but also those in the island's most infamously noisy houses. People whose parties were so loud and frequent that their neighbors rarely had a tranquil night were having their speakers and other music-making paraphernalia turned to toast; and great was their groaning and anger.

The fury of the Silencer's victims was almost, in fact, equal to the joy of everyone who no longer had to suffer the mind-blinding din of the onetime noisemakers.

Moralists wrote letters to the editors, arguing both sides of the issue. The police promised thorough investigations and went through the motions of making them. The victims raged and promised vengeance, and the Silencer worked on, striking where least expected, clothed in darkness, a wraith never seen or heard, and a hero to his people.

Of whom I was one. I loathe bass-booming cars and all other earsplitting modern music. My aversion to such art, in fact, had led some who know me to suspect that I, myself, was the Silencer. It was an honor I could not accept, however much it would have pleased me to do so, for I hadn't the slightest idea how the Silencer did his work.

That Vineyard summer was one of the quietest in memory, for by late June the decibel level of automobile radios and of weekend parties had been lowered considerably all over the island as drivers and hosts sought to avoid the keen-eared Silencer's attention.

At home I gave dark-eyed Zee a husbandly kiss and told her of my conversation with Tony D'Agostine. She laughed. "No wonder the Chief is losing his hair. First the Silencer and now this. The island is becoming a sitcom."

"Life's a jest," I agreed, "but not everyone's amused. The CHOA people are still in a rage about Ron Pierson's castle going up on North Neck."

Zee knew why: "CHOA people want Chappy to be a gated community where nobody can build a new house, especially one bigger than theirs."

Chappaquiddick, the peninsula on the southeast corner of Martha's Vineyard, is home to a few hundred people and some of the finest beaches and fishing spots on the East Coast. CHOA was the Chappaquiddick Home Owners Association, a well-heeled group intent on keeping their bucolic sometimes-island from being invaded by people like Ron Pierson. Or anyone else, for that matter. CHOA also opposed building bike paths for tourists, favored closing East Beach to fishermen and bathers, and, in general, would have preferred it if no one but they, themselves, ever took the little three-car On Time ferry that ran between Chappy Point and the Edgartown Memorial Wharf or drove to Norton's Point Beach, the two modes of getting to Chappy from the rest of Martha's Vineyard.

CHOA's most persistent voice belonged to Maud Mayhew, a lean and lank white-haired aristocrat who had outlasted three husbands and who loathed all changes that had taken place on the Vineyard since the early twentieth century. She belonged to the DAR and to most of the island's conservation organizations, the Garden Club, the Marshal Lea Foundation, CHOA, and probably several other groups of which I was unaware. She wrote almost weekly letters to the local papers protesting development on the Vineyard in general and Chappy in particular, and had something to say at every meeting of every civic or governmental group that might influence change. She had a face like a horse.

"You must admit that Pierson's Palace is going to change the skyline of the bluffs out on North Neck," I said.

Zee nodded. "That's for sure. I don't know how big that house is going to be when he finishes it, but it looks like more space than anybody'd ever need. What is it with these huge houses, anyway?"

"It's been going on forever," I said. "The richest Neanderthal probably had the biggest cave, and Minos had Knossos."

Neither one of us had ever seen Knossos, but we'd read about it and seen pictures. Someday we were going to have to leave Martha's Vineyard and go visit Europe. We were probably the only people on the island who'd never done that.

"Ron Pierson's place may end up bigger than Knossos," said Zee. "By the way, the word is that Ron Pierson has hired Ollie Mattes as a security man. Working nights to keep the lowlife away from the palace. I guess he didn't like having his windows smashed and he fears the anger of CHOA."

"I think CHOA people are the kind who will kill you in court or with looks at a cocktail party, not ambush you in a dark alley."

"Well, somebody trashed the palace's windows the other night, so now Ollie Mattes is on guard to prevent more of such stuff."

"I never thought of Ollie as the security man type," I said. I knew him as a whiner whose wife was long-suffering and whose landscaping business was down the tube because his clients complained that Ollie promised more than he delivered. Ollie was the kind of guy who never saw good in anything or anybody. Everything was tainted, stained, imperfect, worthy of criticism. He seemed permanently unhappy, snide, and suspicious. He was sure that life was a mean experience and that cynicism was the only realistic attitude to take toward it. He made me tired and I avoided him. But I felt sorry for him, too, when I thought of him at all. Like Grendel, he had the curse of Cain upon him and was doomed to journey forever joyless through the swamps of his world.

"Maybe Ron Pierson sees something in him that you don't," said Zee. "Maybe Ollie, being the kind of guy who always expects the worst, is just who you want for a watchman."

That hadn't occurred to me. Maybe there's a place for everyone, even the Ollie Matteses.

"To change to a happier subject," I said, "what say we go for an evening sail tonight? After supper, for a couple of hours? The *Shirley J* hasn't been exercised in a while."

"Sounds good," said Zee, smiling, "and I'm sure the kids won't mind a bit."

The *Shirley J* was our eighteen-foot Herreshoff catboat. We kept it on a stake halfway between the Yacht Club and the Reading Room, two organizations that we had never been invited to join. We kept our dinghy on Collins Beach, chained to a piling of the Reading Room bulkhead so it couldn't be stolen by gentlemen sailors who needed a way to get back to their yachts late at night. I didn't mind their using the dinghy but I did object to them setting it adrift after they were through with it. After the third time local fishermen had found it heading to sea off the Edgartown lighthouse, I'd begun chaining it to the bulkhead.

That evening I rowed Zee and our kids out to the catboat. It had been a soft summer day, and the wind was warm and gentle from the southwest. There was barely a ripple on the waters of the harbor, but just enough wind for us to ghost out into Nantucket Sound and then watch the sun set as we reached Oak Bluffs.

Our son, Joshua, now in the second grade when not at sea, and Diana, his smaller sister, trailed fishing lines over the stern just in case a bluefish was there, and we had a lovely sail. Life on Martha's Vineyard seemed just fine.

As the night came down, we headed home, first on a long reach that took us almost to the Cape Pogue Gut before I began tacking back into Edgartown Harbor.

Thus it was that as we passed offshore of Pierson's Palace atop the North Neck cliffs of Chappaquiddick, Diana, the keen-eyed huntress, pointed through the thickening darkness and said, "What's that, Pa?"

The rest of us looked, but I saw nothing. "What did you see, Diana?"

"Something falling," said my daughter. "I can't see it now."

I stared at the cliffs and at the rocky beach below but still saw nothing. Just then a small gust of wind caught our sail and the *Shirley J* heeled and took my attention away from the shoreline.

We sailed on home under a fingernail moon and the night's first stars, and it wasn't until the following afternoon that I learned that Ollie Mattes had tumbled down the cliff below Pierson's Palace and broken his head on one of the rocks below.

A less important story was that the Silencer had struck again in Oak Bluffs, infuriating the houseful of college kids whose sound system had been melted, but delighting their neighbors.

2

Two days later a well-maintained old pickup came down the long sandy driveway that led to the old hunting and fishing camp that I'd more or less modernized into a year-round house. I dislike NO TRESPASSING signs and thus we don't have any warning to strangers that they're on a private road. The result of this is the occasional lost soul or inquisitive driver who ends up in front of our house and who sometimes, on a sunny day, finds Zee and me taking full-frontal sunbaths in our yard.

On this bright, sunny day I was alone at home, since Zee was at work in the ER of the hospital and our kids were playing with neighbors' kids at their house, but I was not outside improving my all-over tan. I was on our screened front porch working on fishing gear: lubricating reels, sharpening hooks or replacing rusty ones, and making new leaders. Most of the Vineyard bluefish had already gone north, but they'd be back in the fall in time for the fall Bass and Bluefish Derby, and I wanted to be ready for them.

The pickup stopped and a woman got out. I was more than surprised to see that it was the aristocratic Maud Mayhew. To say that Maud and I were usually on the opposite sides of issues would be the understatement of the year.

I watched her as she stared about, taking in the battered old house, the lawn and gardens between the house and the pond, and the view of Sengekontacket Pond and Nantucket Sound, with the Cape Pogue Light in the far distance. She was wearing farming clothes and a floppy-brimmed hat, classic informal dress for owners of acres of land on Chappaquiddick. She walked to the screen door and knocked.

"Come in," I said, and she did. I got up as she squinted at me in the relative darkness of the porch.

"That you, J. W. Jackson?"

"It is. Sit down and tell me what brings you out this way."

She found an old wicker chair that matched mine and lowered herself gingerly into it, the way people do when their joints are getting stiff. I eased back into my own

23

chair as she looked at reels and plugs on the table between us.

"Pays to keep your gear in shape," she said.

"The water around Chappy is littered with lost lures and leaders, and quite a few of them are mine," I said. "I'd just as soon not lose more. And there are a lot of fish still swimming with broken hooks in their mouths."

"Shouldn't fish without proper gear," said Maud. "There ought to be a law."

People often think there should be laws to stop others from doing what they themselves don't do. "Maybe CHOA can talk Beacon Hill into establishing a Plug Police Force," I said. "They can stop everybody going out onto East Beach and toss them in jail if their fishing gear isn't up to snuff."

"Good idea," said Maud, who, like Victoria, was often not amused. "If I wasn't so busy I'd volunteer for the job myself."

"You'd be CHOA's first choice," I said.

"I didn't come here to talk about fishing," said Maud. "I came here to hire you to find out who killed Ollie Mattes."

I put down the plug I was working on before I put a hook through a finger. "Ollie Mattes? I thought Ollie killed himself by falling off the bluff and mashing his head on a rock on the beach."

"Well, apparently you thought wrong. The Chief told me yesterday afternoon that they think now that Ollie got coshed with a blunt instrument before he went over the edge. They think it's homicide."

Had I been in a comic strip, a lightbulb would have gone off in my head. "Ah," I said, "and the suspect list is bound to include the Pierson haters, and you want someone to prove that none of the CHOA people did it."

"No, I want you to prove that my boy Harold didn't do it."

I looked at her for about thirty seconds. Harold Hobbes was her son by her second husband. He was about my age and didn't look a bit like his mother, being tall and handsome in an overweight way. He called himself a farmer because he lived on Maud's farm but actually had no profession, and would have been an insignificant Chappy citizen except that he was Maud's son and therefore rich. He had a reputation as a ladies' man and a fondness for writing angry and loftily worded letters to the local papers protesting the invasion of Chappy by people who weren't members of CHOA. He bored me.

"What makes you think Harold needs help?"

She leaned forward. "Because he was the window breaker. He confessed it to me this morning at breakfast when I told him what the Chief told me yesterday. When he heard that Ollie had been murdered, he panicked and admitted that he'd smashed those windows at Pierson's place. He's afraid that the police will think he went back to do more damage and got caught by Ollie, and that Harold killed him. He's afraid he'll get arrested! He says he's going to go away. I told him that would just make him look more guilty."

The image of Harold going away didn't displease me. "He needs a lawyer," I said. "I imagine you can afford a good one. My advice is that you listen to him and do what he says."

Her long face and big teeth and fierce eyes were those of a wild mare defending her colt. "My son is a coward and a sloth and a bragging womanizer, but he's the only son I have, and I know he's no killer. And I have a lawyer. I have a firm of lawyers. And I'm intelligent enough to do what they advise. But they work in Boston, and they'll need information to handle my son's case if he's charged."

I studied her. "They'll have their favorite private investigators to do that, and the police are trained to solve crimes, so you don't need me for anything. But you know that, so why are you here?"

She gathered herself together, and I could see that being here was terribly hard for her, because, among other reasons, she was an aristocrat and I was without pedigree. I felt a distant touch of sympathy for her. Only a touch. "Because you live here," she said, "and because you were a policeman once. I want somebody who knows this place, who knows how to investigate, and who I can trust!" She spoke through clenched equine teeth.

I gave what she said a semisecond of consideration. "Trust? You and I don't agree about much of anything, and I think your boy Harold is a waste of time. I'm a strange one for you to trust."

She had expected that bullet and she bit it. "Everybody thinks Harold is a waste of time and he probably is, but he's not a killer. You and I may be at each other's throat about keeping people off Chappy, but I've never known you to lie or tell tales. I need an honest man to work for me on this, someone who'll find out the truth and report back to me." She looked around at

27

our battered old house and added, "There'll be money in it. Looks like you could use it."

Her comment about lies showed that she didn't know my character as well as she thought, but she was right about the money. When you live on Martha's Vineyard and you don't have a steady job, you can always use more money.

I gave her a question instead of an answer. "What makes you so sure Harold didn't do it?"

She lifted her chin. "Because I'm his mother. I know him through and through. He's weak. He doesn't have the metal in him to commit murder."

Her vanity roused some pettiness in me and I said, "Cowards and cripples have committed murder, children on the honor roll have killed their kith and kin, dorks have done in other dorks. If you read the papers you know that every other killer has a mother who'll swear he didn't do it and who'll hide him in the bathtub when the cops come after him. What makes Harold different? He has metal enough to be a vandal."

She formed her knobby hands into fists. "He's no killer. I know it!"

I sat back and studied her. Then I said,

"There's something you're not telling me. What is it?"

She glared at me. "I've laid my soul in front of you and you've done nothing but insult me. Go to blazes! I've no more to say to you. I'll find someone else. Damn you!" She opened her hands, placed them on the arms of the chair, and began to push herself erect.

"Where was Harold when Ollie took his fall?" I asked. "He wasn't home, was he?"

The energy went out of her like air from a deflating balloon and she sank back into the chair. I leaned across the table.

"You were home when Ollie bought it, but he wasn't. If he'd been home, you wouldn't be here because you'd be his alibi. Where was he?"

She took a ragged breath and scrubbed her eyes with her hands. "I don't know! He won't tell me! He got home late. I don't know what to do!"

No tears came from her old eyes, but I felt as though some were sliding down her face like raindrops on windowpanes, and I could sense fear behind them.

I got up and went into the house and came back with two cups of black coffee and a glass of cognac. I put a cup in front of each of us and the cognac beside hers.

"Unless you have something against booze," I said, "toss that brandy down in one shot. Don't sip it, toss it down."

She did that and shuddered when the cognac hit her belly, then she dug a handkerchief out of her pocket and dabbed at her lips and eyes. "If we do that during a meal, we call it the Norman Hole," she said. "If you're filled up before the meat course, you toss back a shot of cognac and then you can eat for another hour. I don't usually do it before lunch, though."

"Try some coffee," I said, between sips of my own.

She did that and for a while neither of us spoke. Then I said, "Before you decide that you really want to have some personal private investigator work for you, you should know some possibilities. The first is that he might find out things you don't want to know. He might find evidence that Harold actually is guilty of murder, for instance."

"He isn't. No one will find anything like that. But he needs protection."

"Protection from what? The law? Even if he isn't guilty of murder, he must be involved in something else he doesn't want you to know about. Are you sure you want to know what it is?"

She said nothing, but again I felt fear

emanating from her. I wondered what was under the rock that she didn't want to turn over.

"You want your investigator to report only to you, but if he finds evidence that throws suspicion on Harold, he'll have an obligation to give it to the police. Can you handle that?"

Maternity replied, "You won't find that evidence."

"You're talking like I've agreed to work for you. I haven't. I'm telling you what you need to know if you hire any agent worth his salt. Your detective won't know what he'll find until he looks, and he may not legally be able to keep it confidential. You have to accept that."

She nodded. "I understand. I agree."

"The time may come when you don't. If that happens, you may want your agent to break off the investigation and keep his mouth shut, but he may not want to."

She smiled a hard, horsey smile. "I could fire him. People won't work if they don't get paid."

I shrugged. That was the general rule, but there were exceptions. "Usually not," I said.

"Do we have a deal, then? Will you work for me?"

"I'll tell you something about detectives," I said, looking as far as I could into her eyes. "They expect people to lie to them whenever the people think it serves their interests. They expect the criminals and their friends to lie but they also expect their clients to lie. I expect that you're lying to me right now."

She glared at me. "That's a terribly cynical way to live. I've told you the truth!"

"You haven't told me everything. You haven't told me something I need to know to do this job."

"I *have* told you everything! I'm afraid they'll accuse Harold of killing Ollie Mattes."

"I think you're holding back."

"No! But I need help. I can't protect him myself." She was angry, but her anger, though directed at me, seemed rooted elsewhere. Perhaps in some fear she'd not speak of.

I was suddenly impatient with her. "You'll have to get the help you need somewhere else," I said, "because I won't work with anyone who isn't straight with me."

She had been rich a long time and thought everyone and everything had a price. She swallowed her fury and said,

"We don't have to like each other. Work for me for just a week. Money is no problem. All my husbands had money and I had my own before I married them."

She mentioned an amount and asked if that would cover a week's work. It was considerably more than I'd ever made in any other week, and I wondered if my eyes widened when I heard the figure.

I said, "That's a lot of money, but I'm not interested. I'll give you some advice, though. Whoever works for you will also be working with your lawyers and their investigators and they'll have to cooperate. Your personal investigator will be handicapped if your other people won't talk to him."

She straightened in her chair. "I'll make sure they cooperate with one another. How much money do you want?"

"You can probably buy me if you offer enough," I said, "but I don't feel like being bought. I don't want to work with you. Are you sure you don't mind having people know that you're working to protect Harold? He hasn't been charged with anything, and your friends might wonder why your people are asking questions about him."

"My enemies might wonder the same thing," she said in a bitter, thoughtful voice.

"One last piece of free advice. Don't lie to your people like you're lying to me. They'll expect you to, but don't do it. It won't help your son if he's innocent."

"He is innocent, and I'm not lying!"

I believed half of that. "If you say so. There's a very good private investigation organization in Boston called Thornberry Security. I suggest that you give them a call."

She pushed herself out of her chair. "You're probably right to refuse this job," she said. "We've never gotten along before and we probably wouldn't if you went to work for me. I'm sorry to have wasted your time."

I stood. "I hope your son is innocent."

She inclined her hoary, horsey head. "Thank you for your time." She turned away, then turned suddenly back and surprised me by bursting into tears. "Please help me!" she cried. "Please! I need your help. Don't turn me away!"

I was shocked into pity. I saw my hands go out and touch her shaking shoulders and pull her close. My arms went around her and I heard my voice say, all on its own, as if at a distance, "All right. All right. I'll do what I can. Don't worry. Don't worry."

She was tough, and after a while she pulled away, embarrassed. "Sorry. I hate emotional people."

"Don't be sorry." I went into the house and came out with a clean handkerchief. She blew her nose and wiped her red eyes. "Thank you."

"I'll come over tomorrow and talk with Harold. With luck we'll find out where he was when Ollie was killed."

I watched her drive away and wondered if I should have taken the job. I didn't like Harold Hobbes, but on the other hand, the money was good and a murder involving the rich or famous is always a thought teaser.

The next morning, as I listened to the local news on WMVY, I learned that Norton's Point Beach was going to be closed that very day by the Fish and Wildlife experts, that the busy Silencer had struck again in Oak Bluffs, and that the island had suffered a second homicide within the week. Harold Hobbes had been found bludgeoned to death in his own driveway. His mother, Maud Mayhew, returning home from a CHOA meeting the previous evening, had found the body and phoned the police.

3

As I read of Harold Hobbes's death, I experienced a powerful feeling of guilt, as though I were somehow responsible. The irrationality of this notion annoyed me as much as the feeling itself. I pushed it away, but it was instantly replaced by an equally irrational and powerful feeling of duty, of obligation to discover who had done this to a man I'd promised to protect. He was an old woman's only son. She must be devastated. I pushed at this feeling, too, but with no effect, because I could imagine my own emotions if anything should happen to Joshua or Diana.

Still, I attempted to do away with my guilt through action. I finished refurbishing our fishing gear, did some repairs on the tree house with the help of Joshua and Diana and the supervision of the two cats, Oliver Underfoot and Velcro, and even climbed on our roof and made another search for the source of the persistent leak in the corner of the living room that dripped every time we had a wet northeaster. Naturally I couldn't find it because you can never find a leak that's not leaking at that moment. Annoying. Even more annoying was the fact that all my busywork failed to ease my mind, so just before noon I gave up, loaded the kids into my rusty Land Cruiser, and drove to the Edgartown police station.

Four-year-old Diana the huntress was always pleased to go for a ride, especially if it eventually led to something to eat. She had gotten that sobriquet, in fact, because of her seemingly permanent search for food. One meal was scarcely over before she was ready for the next one. A dark-haired, dark-eyed miniature of her slender mother, she could eat like a horse and never show it.

Big brother Joshua also liked to go for rides, but he was less insistent on a culinary reward at journey's end. For him the ride was enough in itself, for he was a transportation buff who liked cars, boats, bikes, planes, and all other known vehicles. It was a fascination I could not grasp, nor could I guess the gene pool from which it came. All children are mysteries in one way or another.

"Pa?"

"Yes, Diana."

"Can we get ice cream?"

How predictable. "Sure. But first I have to talk with the Chief."

At the station I left my offspring playing crazy eights in the backseat of the truck and went inside.

The Chief's office was full of cops, including Sergeant Dom Agganis of the state police. I guessed they were discussing the recent unpleasantness on Chappaquiddick. In Massachusetts, the state police handle all homicide investigations outside Boston, which has its own homicide people. This can create tension between the state cops and the local cops, who often know more about the particulars of a crime than the state cops do.

Fortunately for Edgartown, Dom Agganis and the Chief got along very well. Fortunately for me, I got along with both Dom and the Chief. The only cop in the office that I didn't get along with was Dom's second-in-command, Officer Olive Otero. Olive and I had never, ever hit it off. We were like flint and steel; the first time we met, sparks flew and they'd flown ever since. Why that was, I could not say. Nor, I guessed, could Olive. Olive saw me come toward the Chief's office and tried to push the door shut in my face. I got a sandal out just in time to stop it.

"This is a meeting of police," said Olive, giving my foot a kick with her shiny black shoe and shoving harder on the door.

Dom Agganis, hearing his subordinate's voice, turned and put his big hand on the door. "Olive is correct," he said. "Your business will have to wait a few minutes."

"If you're talking about Harold Hobbes," I said, "I might have something you can use."

"I doubt that," said Olive.

"Find a chair," said Dom. "I'll be out in a few minutes."

Olive sneered and shut the door.

I looked at Kit Goulart, who was behind the reception desk and listening to every word. Kit was over six feet tall and the size of a horse. Her husband was of the same dimensions. Together they made a team that could probably outpull a yoke of oxen.

"Round one goes to Otera," said Kit. She pointed to a bench against the wall. "Go to a neutral corner and when the bell rings, come out fighting."

Instead I took a peek at my truck. The kids were still playing. Crazy eights is a good game for all ages. I turned back to Kit.

"Has the law collected Mickey Gomes, or is he still on the loose?"

"Oh, they collected him, all right. He was just where they figured he'd be: hiding in the woods behind the girl's house and getting hungry."

"He hasn't broken out again?"

"No, they took away his screwdriver and replaced the screen with bars on his favorite escape window, so Mickey will be staying put for a while, much to his girlfriend's disappointment, no doubt."

"Don't her parents object to him coming around all the time and getting their daughter pregnant?"

"The rape was only statutory. I guess they figure that if Mickey's willing to break jail every week or so to see their little girl, his love is true and the child-to-be is the proof."

"It's nice to know that romance is not dead, but I imagine the wedding will be delayed until Mickey serves the extra time he'll get for busting out."

Kit nodded. "The child will no doubt emerge into the outer world before Mickey does."

"Tell me something. How come he never escaped until after supper and always came back before breakfast? Was that because he figured his keepers would be asleep between meals?"

"Ah," said Kit, "a sound but incorrect theory. The real reason is Duane Miller. You must have heard about him. There was a story about him in the *Gazette* a while back."

"But of course."

It all came back to me. Duane Miller was a gourmet chef who was serving a term in jail for selling dope to some friends. He'd made a deal with the jailers: if they'd use the jail's food money to buy groceries he ordered, he'd cook for both the inmates and their keepers. The result of the agreement was that the best food on Martha's Vineyard was served in the county jail. No wonder Mickey made sure that he never missed a meal inside.

"You should write a book called *Jail Tales*," I said. "It would be true, but everyone would believe it was fiction."

"When I write my book, I'm going to call it *Policing Paradise*," said Kit. "No one who isn't a cop will believe what I say either, but I won't have to make anything up. I understand that one or two guys who used to work over at the jail have gotten through."

On the Vineyard, when you're no longer

working at a job, you're said to have "gotten through." The phrase includes no indication of causality. If Joe Blow got fired or quit, you'd know something about what happened, but if he got through, you wouldn't. I liked that. In the case of the ex-jailers who had now gotten through, you might guess that they'd gotten fired because they'd allowed Mickey Gomes to escape over and over again, but you couldn't be sure. Maybe they'd quit so they could go back to grad school to finish their doctoral studies.

Behind me a loud mumble of voices indicated that the Chief's office door had opened, and I turned to see Dom Agganis waving me inside as other officers moved out.

I peeked at the kids as I went that way and saw that they were still being good enough to be rewarded with ice cream when I rejoined them. Inside the office I found myself with Dom, Olive, and the Chief.

"Well?" The Chief was turning his unlit pipe in his hands. He was hoping, I thought, that my visit would be brief so he could duck outside and light up. I didn't blame him. I hadn't smoked in years but I still missed my bent corncob.

"You've talked with Maud Mayhew, of course," I said. "Did she mention paying me a visit yesterday?"

The Chief and the state cops exchanged glances that didn't reveal a thing. "Tell me about it," he said.

"She hired me to prove that Harold didn't kill Ollie Mattes."

This time the Chief's eyes narrowed slightly. He stuck the cold pipe in his mouth and chewed on the stem for a moment, then said, "Why did she think he needed somebody to do that?"

"Because, according to Maud, Harold told her he'd smashed the windows in the Pierson house and he was afraid that if that got out he'd be suspected of going back there again and killing Ollie."

Silence prevailed. Finally Dom Agganis said, "Maud didn't mention talking with you. Did you take the job?"

"Yes. I suggested she get in touch with Thornberry Security, up in Boston, but she talked me into it."

"Are you sure you understood her right about Harold being the window breaker?"

"There wasn't much to misunderstand."

"It wouldn't be hard for you," said Olive. "You could misunderstand a soup spoon."

"Why didn't you tell us what Maud said

as soon as you heard it?" asked Dom.

"I didn't like Harold Hobbes but I couldn't see him as a killer. I wasn't going to drop a dime on him for breaking Pierson's windows, especially when I was trying to keep him from being nailed as Ollie's killer."

"If you'd spoken up, he might be alive today," said Olive. "We might have been talking with him when he got his head bashed in. You're a sad case, Jackson. I've got half a notion to collar you for withholding evidence of a crime."

"Try to control your attack puppy here, Dom," I said. "She's liable to get so excited she'll bite herself to death."

"Both of you calm down," said Dom, stepping between us. "I'm sick of this business between you two. You want to badmouth each other, you do it on your own time, not mine! You got that?"

"I'm a civilian," I said. "I'm civil by definition. I'm kind, loyal, and patriotic. My only flaw is that I don't like small dogs." I looked at Olive. "Including this one."

Olive clenched her teeth but said nothing.

"Olive's right, you know," said the Chief. "If you'd told us what Maud told you, we might have had a talk with Hobbes and

44

maybe he'd be alive instead of dead."

"That's why I'm here now. I had that same idea stuck in my brain. I don't believe it, but I had a hard time getting rid of it. Anyway, I thought it might interest you to know about Harold claiming to be the window breaker. It might save you some sleuthing."

The Chief nodded. "We'll talk to Maud about it. You have any other tips you want to pass along?"

"Only that Harold apparently had a life Maud didn't know about. He wouldn't tell her where he was when Ollie was killed. Or maybe he did tell her but she just didn't want to tell me. Maybe she'll tell you."

The Chief looked at me steadily. "You aren't thinking of getting involved in this business, are you?"

"Maud hired me to help Harold."

"You're not answering my question."

"Harold's dead, so you could argue that my job's over."

"Stop dancing. Just answer the question."

"I go over to Chappy pretty often this time of year. I'll probably keep it up."

"Don't interfere with our work."

"I gave up being a cop years ago. I don't want your job."

45

"Do you think Maud knows more than she told you about Harold?"

"I believe people will hold back information and lie to defend themselves and the ones they love. I accused Maud of doing that, hoping that it might shock her into telling me more than she did. But she didn't shock and I can't think of any reason why she would have lied to me, although maybe she did. Do you have any theories about who coshed Harold?"

"None of your business," said Olive.

"We're working on it," said the Chief. "You think you owe something to Maud, do you? Your long nose is itchy, isn't it?"

"My nose isn't itchy," I said, "but I owe Maud. Or maybe it's Harold I owe. Or maybe Olive is right for once: maybe none of this is my business. I've told you everything I know, and now I'm going to take my kids down for ice cream. You minions of the law can take it from here."

I turned and went out the door. As I did, I heard the Chief's ironic voice say, "And why so great a no?"

He'd been reading *Cyrano* again, apparently. That also explained the itchy nose metaphor.

I got into the Land Cruiser and said, "Who won the game?"

46

"We're not through yet, Pa." One of the nice things about crazy eights is that it can go on a long, long time; maybe forever.

"What do you guys say to us getting some ice cream first and then taking a ride over to Chappaquiddick?"

Diana the huntress folded her cards immediately. I wasn't surprised. "That sounds good, Pa! Let's do it."

And we did. We went to Mad Martha's and got cones, then, eating till the cones were gone, took the On Time ferry across to Chappy and drove to the fishermen's parking lot above Cape Pogue Gut on North Neck, where we parked beside a couple of other cars decorated with rod racks.

"Are we going fishing, Pa?" asked Joshua as we got out of the truck.

"No. We're going to take a walk along the beach and look at a new house that's being built on top of the bluffs."

4

On North Neck there's a path leading from the small fishermen's parking lot to the top of the bluffs overlooking Cape Pogue Gut, and a stairway leading down to the beach. Fishermen who don't have four-wheel-drive vehicles or lack the time to drive all the way out to the far beaches of Chappaquiddick can park in the lot and walk to the gut to do their fishing. A lot of fish have been caught in the gut, some of them by me.

When the idea of the lot was first proposed to the town selectmen, a number of North Neck homeowners howled to the moon. The neighborhood's ambience was going to be ruined by hordes of fishermen; ecological disaster would occur; the end of the world was at hand. Lawsuits were threatened; pious arguments were printed in the local papers; people who had their own stairways down the bluffs condemned the proposed stairway as a threat to the environment; searches for endangered plants and insects were demanded. Great was the hue and cry of CHOA people and others.

But all in vain. The town held firm and built the lot, path, and stairway, and, lo, the sun continued to rise in the east, North Neck land prices did not plummet, and the cry of the turtle was still heard throughout the land.

From the top of the bluffs, Joshua and Diana and I had a good view of the gut. There were a couple of fly casters working the water on our side, and on the other side three SUVs were parked. Their drivers and passengers were also casting into the fast-moving stream that was flowing into Cape Pogue Pond as the tide rose. I'd sailed in and out of the pond many times, and it could be very tough going if you were tacking against a strong tide and a weak wind.

To the north, beyond the Cape Pogue elbow and across the edge of Nantucket Sound, we could see the Oak Bluffs bluffs and beyond them, running to the east, the dim line of land that was Cape Cod. To the west was Edgartown, with its white lighthouse looking small against the higher background of houses on Starbuck Neck. There were sailboats on the blue sound and as always I wondered whither they were bound.

Immediately to our left the bluff was topped by houses, all of them modest when compared with the rising skeleton of Ron Pierson's mansion-in-progress. I was of two minds about the building of palaces on the Vineyard. On the one hand I wished their owners would settle for something simpler, but on the other I thought they had the right to build any size house they wanted to build.

My disapproval of some people telling other people what size houses they should live in was no doubt a by-product of my general dislike of people in positions of authority ever trying to tell me what to do and how to do it. The more commandingly they behaved, the less kindly I took to such folk and the more sympathetic I was to those half-mad hermits who go off and live in caves.

We went down the stairs and walked west, with the bluffs rising on our left and the waves slapping the shore on our right. It didn't take long to fetch the rocky stretch of beach below Pierson's Palace, where Ollie Mattes's body had been found three days ago lying among the stones.

I looked up at the steep bluff down

which Diana had seen something falling as we'd come home from our evening sail. It was easy to imagine how the person who had caved in Ollie's head and tossed his body off the cliff might have hoped, even expected, that the death would have been ruled an accident. But as has happened with better plans than that one, the medical examiner had seen through it and now Ollie's murderer was being sought by the local law.

"You two stay down here," I said to my offspring. "I'm going up to the top."

"Oh, good! We'll come too!"

"No, you won't. I don't want to worry about you falling down and breaking your necks. You wait here."

"We won't break our necks, Pa. We're good climbers."

Better than I was, probably, but I was firm.

"Stay here until I get back."

"What if you fall down and break your neck?"

It was not an entirely unlikely possibility. "Then you go back to the gut and get some help from those fishermen. But don't worry. I'm not going to fall, and I won't be long."

"Whatcha gonna do up there, Pa?"

51

"Just look around."

The slope was made of dirt and stone brought down from New Hampshire and points north by the last ice age glacier. The islands of Nantucket, Martha's Vineyard, Block Island, and Long Island marked the southern end of its progress. All had once been only hills of earth piled up by the ice, but as the glaciers melted and the sea rose they had become islands.

The bluff was very hard going, and I had to climb carefully because of the treacherous footing. More than once I came close to sliding back down to the beach, and I wished for one of those staircases that led down the bluff from some of the older North Neck homes. Ron Pierson would no doubt have such a stairway of his own someday, but he didn't have one today. Where are you when I need you, Ron? As I climbed I was glad that I didn't have to do it during the rain or during the night, and I wondered just what it was I thought I might find at the top of the bluff.

When I reached it, I glanced down and saw that Joshua was showing Diana how to skip flat rocks across the water. It was a good thing to know, and I was pleased that my son was teaching his sister how it was done. Then I peeked over the lip of the cliff to see if anyone — workman, watchman, policeman, or other person — was there. No one was, but yellow police tape surrounded the partially built house and part of the grounds. I scrambled to my feet and studied the place.

A new driveway had been bulldozed through the trees, and trees and oak brush had been cut down to create a broad open space for the house and future lawns and outbuildings. Construction materials, both of stone and wood, were stacked everywhere, and a trailer for tools and other equipment was parked beside a large generator. I was alone on the grounds and aware of that odd silence you sometimes hear around an empty or unfinished structure. I guessed that the yellow tape was keeping workers away and that Pierson hadn't yet had time to find himself another watchman to keep an eye on things.

The first story of the house and part of the second were already closed in, and a third story had been framed. A wide porch surrounded the house and a large second-story balcony faced the sea. The house was being built in a Victorian style more typical of Oak Bluffs than of Edgartown, and it was going to be huge.

Every window in the house seemed to

have been broken, including the leaded, stained-glass panes of a miniature version of the Chartres rose window over the front door. It had taken a good deal of time to do all that damage and must have made a certain amount of noise. I wondered if any of the neighbors had heard anything.

I ducked under the police tape and went into the house. Even though it was in the early stages of construction, I could see that it was going to be a first-class structure, with no money being spared by its owner. There was a massive cellar space, and a carved and curved staircase led to the second floor. The kitchen was big enough for a half dozen cooks, and its stove, refrigerator, freezer, sinks, and cabinets, all still in their boxes, were the finest made. There were two boxed dishwashers and the counters were topped with stone.

I went through the place from top to bottom, touching nothing but the occasional doorknob. I couldn't be sure, but the faucets in the bathrooms seemed to be made of gold.

I walked around the porch and looked at the grounds, wondering where watchman Ollie Mattes had encountered his nemesis. There was no way for me to tell. One thing was certain, though: there were blunt instruments aplenty near at hand, in the form of tools and lengths of wood and pipe.

I thought about Ollie Mattes, and about the gold faucets, and about Harold Hobbes.

Then I heard the sound of a vehicle coming up the driveway, and trotted back to the lip of the bluff, where I slid down out of sight then peeked back over. J. W. Jackson, master spy. The vehicle was a middle-aged station wagon driven by a woman. She parked and got out and looked at the house. I guessed she was about forty, but I can never really tell how old people are these days. Thanks to clothing styles, hair dye and makeup, diet, exercise, and plastic surgery, some daughters look older than their mothers, and some fathers look younger than their sons.

This woman's blonde hair was shoulder length and she was wearing casual clothes that were not new but that had been expensive when purchased. Two of the ways you can tell the difference between rich girls and poor girls is that poor girls have long hair and rich girls don't, and that poor girls like to wear the newest clothes they can afford and rich girls don't. Another difference is that rich girls walk like they're carrying field-hockey sticks and poor girls don't. Rich girls also have bigger chins a lot of the time but that didn't apply in this case. This woman's chin was normal, but there was no doubt that she was a rich girl.

I didn't know who she was, but then I don't know most of the people on Martha's Vineyard, especially the rich girls. I memorized the license plate on the station wagon then ducked down as the woman took her eyes off the house and swung them in my direction. It seemed a good time to retreat, so I did that, stepping carefully and doing some sliding down the slope, preceded by bouncing stones and small avalanches of dirt and sand. On the beach I dusted myself off and joined my children at the water's edge.

Diana had not mastered the art of skipping stones and was getting tired of trying.

Part of her problem was that her stones weren't flat enough. Nobody can skim a round rock. I found some flat ones.

"Here," I said, giving her one that was the right size for her little hand. "My father called these 'donies' when I was a kid. When we threw rocks he called it flinging donies. We called slingshots donie flingers.

This game was called skipping donies. Watch the way Joshua is doing it. See? He throws sidearm and he rolls the donie off his trigger finger. Like this." I showed her how to hold the donie, then flung it and watched it skip four times. "Now you try it."

She did but got no skips. I gave her another donie and wrapped her hand around it. "Hook your trigger finger around the edge like this, and throw it so the flat side hits the water."

She flipped it and it skipped. "I did it!" She was happy.

I looked up toward the top of the bluff. The woman was outlined against the sky, looking down. I waved and she moved back out of sight.

As we walked back toward the fishermen's stairway, Diana flung some more donies. Some of them skipped and some of them didn't. Joshua and I flung some, too, and also had both successes and failures. So it goes in the donie-flinging game. Now and then I found a way to glance back at Ron Pierson's palace, but I saw no more of the woman.

"Flinging donies is fun, Pa!" Diana was very pleased.

"Yes, it is. From now on you'll always be

able to skip them. It's a good talent to have."

Back in Edgartown I stopped by the police station again. The Chief, no longer surrounded by other lawmen, was in his office doing paperwork, his least favorite professional activity. He would much have preferred to be out investigating his town's two killings, but such is not the fate of police chiefs. He was, understandably, in a sour mood. I didn't improve it any when I asked him to tell me who belonged to the license plate number of the station wagon.

"Why do you want to know?"

"I'm just curious. But don't tell me if it makes you grumpy. I can find out some other way."

"I'll be grumpy if I feel like it."

"Okay, okay. Good-bye."

"Sit back down."

He went out and came back and handed me a scrap of paper. Even I recognized the name on it. It belonged to one of the Vineyard's socially elite families, the Bradfords, whose members were often featured in both the island's and Boston's newspapers. The Bradfords lived in Chilmark, where people talk a lot about affordable housing but the town doesn't have any. Chilmarkians are not, of course, the only

58

Vineyarders to give lip service to the needs of the poor, as long as they live in some other neighborhood.

"You're involving yourself in lofty social circles," said the Chief. "Why are you interested in Cheryl Bradford's Volvo?"

I had prepared my lie. "The kids and I were over on North Neck checking out the fishing. When we came back I saw the car headed into that driveway that leads out to Ron Pierson's new place. I wondered who was going in there, that's all. Is Cheryl Bradford a relative of Pierson's or something?"

He didn't answer. Instead, he said, "How do you know it was Pierson's driveway?"

"It's the only new driveway leading off the North Neck road, and it heads in the direction of Pierson's house. Why do you suppose Cheryl Bradford is interested in Ron Pierson's house?"

"Maybe for the same reason you're interested in her car. Nosiness. Or maybe she just wanted to eyeball the scene of the crime. In any case, nobody else but workmen will be going in there from now on because Ron Pierson is shipping down some company security men for a twenty-four-hour palace guard. They'll get here

59

this afternoon, I'm told."

"Too bad he didn't do that in the first place."

"Yeah. Now, unless you have something else for me to do, I'll get back at this paperwork. Ever since we got computers I've had more paperwork than ever." It was a familiar complaint, but one I didn't make because I was the last person in the Western world without a computer.

"Do the Bradfords and the Mayhews pal around?" I asked.

"You'll have to ask the Bradfords and the Mayhews, but most of these old island families have known each other for generations."

"Do they get along with each other?"

The Chief leaned back in his chair. "Most people get along most of the time. What's gotten you interested in the local aristocrats?"

I ticked off my points on my fingers. "Ron Pierson owns the house where Ollie Mattes got himself killed. Harold Hobbes trashed the windows of the house and Maud thought he'd be accused of killing Ollie. Now Harold's dead and Cheryl Bradford appears on the scene. We've got a Mayhew, a Hobbes, a Pierson, and a Bradford. Those are the names of four richer-than-Croesus families who seem to have ties to at least one murder and maybe two."

"We don't have any official evidence that there's a link between the killings, and we won't have until we get the ME's report on Harold Hobbes. But, it may surprise you to learn that we small-town cops have already noticed that some island money seems to be involved in these cases. I'll add Cheryl Bradford's name to my list of people to talk to. Thanks for the information and good-bye. Unless you want to stay and do this paperwork. Interested?"

"No." I got up.

"I can make you a special officer, so it'll be legal."

"Not a chance. I've already been a cop once and I have no interest in being one again." I went out the door and got into the Land Cruiser.

"Pa."

"What, Joshua?"

"You know how you won't let us have a dog?"

"That's right. No dogs. I know all your friends have them, but we're not going to get one. We already have Oliver Underfoot and Velcro, and two cats are all the animals we're going to have."

"And you know how you won't let us have a ferret, either?" asked Diana.

"That's right, too. No ferrets."

"Pa."

"What?"

"Can we get a computer? All our friends have them."

5

At supper the computer question was raised again.

"They have computers at school, Pa. We use them there all the time." The children traded looks and nods as they chewed.

I frowned at Diana. "Do you really have them at preschool?"

"Yes, Pa. We have several. I like the green one best."

I didn't know they made green computers.

"We have them at the hospital," said Zee in her most reasonable voice.

"I've lived all my life without a computer," I said. "I don't need one."

"The children could use it for their schoolwork."

"Yeah, Pa!"

"You kids are doing just fine in school. Besides, I want you to read books, not look at a computer."

"We'd still read books, Pa."

"We don't have an answering machine or a color TV either. I imagine you'll want those too. What'll be next?"

"A color TV would be good, Pa!"

I chewed my pork sate and had some wine.

"This is the twenty-first century, you know," said Zee, looking at me with her big dark bottomless eyes.

"This is Martha's Vineyard," I said. "When the wind blows the wrong way the electricity goes out. What are you going to do with all your electrical gadgets when that happens? Your worlds will end."

"The electricity always comes back on again, Jefferson."

Zee's voice was reasonable but firm. I chewed some more.

"All right," I said. "I'll think about it. Not about a color TV. Nobody needs a color TV. I'll think about a computer. If you kids really need it for school."

"We do, Pa!"

The children and their mother smiled at one another. As far as they were concerned, it was a done deal.

"I'll talk with the people at the Computer Lab," I said. "I don't know anything at all about computers."

"I'll go with you when you do," said Zee. "I know how to turn one on, at least."

"We'll come too, Pa. We'll show you how to use them. It's not hard." Joshua spoke as if to a child.

Diana the huntress, ever pursuing food, ate her last bite of sate. "Pa, can I have some more, please?"

"Certainly." I handed her the serving dish and she took another skewer of pork. Someday she herself or someone else was going to have to feed a grown-up Diana. I didn't envy that person's grocery bill.

When the children were in bed, Zee and I took over the living room sofa. For background music we played our tape of Beverly Sills and company singing arias from *La Traviata*. Beverly's voice was like a flute, and I once again agreed with myself that she would be a member of the Jackson Quintet, which would consist of me, Emmylou Harris, Pavarotti, Beverly, and Willie Nelson. Emmylou, Willie, and I would play guitar and all of us would sing.

"I think it'll be good for Joshua and Diana to have a computer," said Zee, lying down and putting her head in my lap. "On another subject, they tell me that you were all over on Chappy this morning and that you scaled a cliff while they skipped donies in the water. We never called them donies when I was a girl, by the way."

There are few secrets in a small family. I told her about my day.

"Why are you so interested in all that Chappy business?" she asked.

I gave her the only reason I could think of: irrational guilt.

"Well," she said, "you and absurdity are not unknown companions, so I can accept that. Since you've obviously been thinking about all the goings-on, what do you make of the Chappy news, aside from that it's bad?"

"I don't know enough to have any opinions worth talking about, but if I were a betting man I'd put a week's salary that there's a link between the two killings."

"A pretty cheap bet, Jefferson, since you don't work for a salary. What's the link?"

"I don't know the real link, but they were both coshed with blunt instruments and both were killed in the early evening."

"That's not much. Where is your hand going?"

"No, it isn't, but it's been years since anybody got murdered on Chappy and now we've had two killings in less than a week. Seems quite a coincidence. And my hand isn't going anywhere."

"Coincidences happen all the time. Yes, it is."

"If we were in a western I could say I just have a hunch. Hunches are what we manly men have instead of intuition. You women have all the intuition."

"We're not in a western, Jeff. Do you have a hunch, anyway?" She slapped at my hand. "No tickling!"

I took the offending hand away from her ribs and placed it on her right breast, one of my two favorites. She put her hand over mine. "Half a hunch, at least," I said. "Another thing: the only way to drive to Pierson's house is on that new driveway. That's the way Cheryl Bradford got there and that's the only way anybody else would get there unless they wanted to climb the bluff like I did or cut through the scrub oak and green brier on some neighbor's land. I can't imagine Harold Hobbes scaling the bluff or getting himself scratched up going through the woods, so I think he probably used the driveway. There wasn't any guard there at the time, so after he did his work, he left the same way."

"You're just guessing, of course."

"It isn't good for a wife to be so skeptical of her husband's thoughts," I said. "You should remember that women are creatures of passion, not intellect. You ladies should leave the brain work to us guys."

"I'm sure you'll pardon me while I laugh myself to death. You're a real card, Jeff. You have busy fingers, too."

"Busy fingers indicate a busy mind. Anyway, I'm also guessing that whoever did in Ollie Mattes probably came in that way, too. Ollie got killed at dusk and climbing that bluff in bad light would have been tough for his killer. The same for going through the woods."

"Meaning that Ollie saw him in plenty of time and wasn't taken by surprise."

"Exactly. I don't know if Ollie put up a fight. If he did, the killing might have been unintentional. Maybe the other guy wouldn't leave and they struggled and Ollie got his head bashed in in the general course of things."

"And when the guy saw that Ollie was dead, he panicked and pitched him over the bluff to make it look like Ollie'd killed himself in the fall." Zee pursed her lips. "I wonder if Ollie had a cell phone. Seems like he should have, being all alone out there like that."

"I'll have to ask." There were a lot of things I didn't know.

"Because if he did and didn't use it,"

68

said Zee, "it could mean that whoever killed him was somebody he knew and wasn't afraid of. Because if this other guy was a stranger or gave him trouble, it seems to me that he'd have called the cops."

That right breast was a good one, all right. I unbuttoned the top of her blouse and said, "He would have if he'd had time and didn't think he could handle the situation himself. He might have thought he didn't need any help." I slipped my hand inside the blouse. She wasn't wearing a bra. Her breathing changed.

"This talk is full of ifs and guesses," she said, running her tongue over her lips.

"There are a couple of things I'm pretty sure of," I said, moving my fingers gently. "One is that Harold Hobbes didn't trash all those windows alone. There were too many of them. He'd have had to be there for hours, and I don't think he had the nerve to hang around that long."

"What's the other thing?"

"It's that I'm getting very disinterested in the subject of this conversation. I have something else in mind."

"It's not all in your mind, Jeff. My pillow is getting a lump."

"That's where I keep my mind," I said, running my hand south over her flat belly.

She loosened her belt and reached for mine as we abandoned the couch for the rug on the floor. Chappy and its troubles disappeared from my consciousness.

"I think that God must be bisexual," said Zee a half hour later as we lay breathless and sweaty, wrapped in each other's arms like the griefs of the ages.

"This will come as bad news to the Southern Baptists," I said when I finished running my tongue over that magic place just at the base of her throat. "What brings you to that conclusion?"

Her arms tightened around me. "Because all participants feel joy, regardless of gender."

"You have a point."

She held my hand but rolled over onto her back and looked at the ceiling where our fishing rods were hung as rods had been hung since my father had bought the place decades before.

"Of course," she said, "Puritans look upon pleasure as a sign of sin."

"That probably doesn't keep them from sex," I said. "Remember Byron."

"Yes, poor Byron. It's bad to have a religious upbringing that doesn't keep you from sinning but does keep you from enjoying it as much as you should. It's a familiar song, I'm afraid, but I'm glad to say it's not one you or I sing." She squeezed my fingers and flashed me a white, sensual, feline smile.

"Obscenity the Puritans," I said.

"It would probably be good for them," agreed Zee. "Did you know that Cheryl Bradford has a brother?"

"A Puritan brother?"

"No. I'm changing the subject. Her brother is sort of like one of those militia types you read about who live out in Idaho in log cabins. Only this one lives in West Tisbury."

"Where'd you learn about this guy?" I asked.

"From Cheryl. Then, once she'd told me, I heard it some more. You know how it is: you've never heard of something; then as soon as you finally do, you hear about it all the time."

"How'd you happen to be talking with Cheryl Bradford?"

"I work in the ER at the hospital, remember? I meet a lot of people, including Bradfords. Cheryl's daughter Annie Pease got tossed off her horse into some barbed wire a while back. Cheryl brought the girl in and we stitched her up and they took her home."

71

"How old was the girl?"

"She was about sixteen then. She's at Harvard now. All the Bradford women used to go to Vassar, but now there isn't any Vassar so they go to Harvard."

"I thought Harvard only took the intellectually elite."

"You obviously never dated any Harvard men."

"You got me there. Cheryl Bradford doesn't look old enough to have a daughter at Harvard."

"Neither do you, but you are."

"How come Cheryl Bradford is still a Bradford if she has a daughter named Annie Pease? Didn't she marry the girl's dad?"

"She went back to being a Bradford when her husband died. But Annie was born a Pease and still is one."

"What was the husband's name?"

"George Pease, as in Pease's Point Way. If you believe that story about Europeans settling on the Vineyard before 1642, the Peases have been here longer than the Mayhews, even."

"Maud Mayhew went back to her maiden name, too, after all three of her marriages ended. It must be a habit among local upper-class ladies. I take it that Annie

Pease survived her horse wreck without too much damage."

"The Bradfords are tough," said Zee. "They've owned that farm of theirs for a long time and they use horse liniment to cure their wounds most of the time. Anyway, while the girl was being stitched up, Cheryl mentioned her brother Ethan. He'd been riding with the girl when the accident happened and had brought her back to the house."

"Uncle Ethan, the hermit. Why doesn't he stay on the old homestead?"

"His mother likes her horses better than she likes him, I gather. A very crusty lady. When he brought Annie to the house, his mother was so furious with him that Ethan fled the farm to save his hide. Cheryl says he has a cabin in the wilds of West Tisbury and spends his time trying to avoid the twentieth century. He eats fish and jacked deer and whatever he can grow in his garden or find in the woods. Do you think the kids are asleep?"

"If the noise we've been making hasn't gotten them out here to see what's been going on, I'd say they must be asleep. Why?"

"This is why," she said, and rolled back toward me.

6

The next morning Zee wasn't working, so I left her and the kids and went to the Edgartown Police Station. The Chief looked up from his desk when I darkened his door.

"Just one question," I said. "Did Ollie Mattes have a cell phone with him that evening when he was killed?"

"Why do you want to know?"

"Do you always answer a question with another one?"

"Why shouldn't I? I get paid to ask questions."

"Well, did he?"

"Why do you want to know?"

I sighed as theatrically as I could. "I'd like to know why he didn't call you guys when whoever coshed him showed up."

He tapped his ballpoint pen on the desk. "The question occurred to us, too. I don't know why he didn't call, although I can think of several reasons why he might not have."

"So he did have a cell phone."

"Any ideas about why he didn't use it?"

"None that you haven't already thought about. Do you know anything about Ethan Bradford?"

"You said you had just one question. Isn't Ethan that guy up in West Tisbury who lives in a tent or something? The one who used to work for Raytheon or some such outfit before he decided that he'd rather be a hermit?"

"That sounds like the guy."

"What about him?"

"He's Cheryl Bradford's brother. You ever see him around Edgartown?"

The Chief studied me. "Everybody comes to Edgartown at one time or another. If you sit in front of the town hall long enough you'll see the Queen of England go by. What's so interesting about Ethan Bradford aside from the fact that you saw his sister on Chappaquiddick?"

"You said that all the old island families know one another. What I've heard about Ethan is that he'd prefer it if we were still in an earlier century instead of this one, which makes me think he might not be happy about our current boom in castle building."

"And you think that might make him more likely than most to cosh other people."

"Those are your words, not mine, Chief. While we're discussing old island families, though, what can you tell me about George Pease? Cheryl Bradford was married to him."

The Chief cocked his head slightly to one side. "George got his head kicked in by a horse. It's what you get by marrying into one of those equestrian families like the Bradfords. Happened in the family barn, as I recall. I think that eliminates him as a suspect in this case, if you were giving him consideration."

"I guess I'll scratch him off my list. How did the widow take the loss?"

"I don't keep track of the lives and times of the island's elite. You'll have to ask somebody else about Cheryl's emotional crises, if she has any."

"Did she remarry?"

He shrugged. "Not that I know of. Maybe those people who write the Chilmark columns in the *Gazette* or the *Times* can tell you. Now go away. I've got work to do."

I said good-bye and left.

I think of myself as being as gossipy as

76

most people, but in this case as in others I was forced to admit that I apparently hadn't kept track of the doings of the island's important people. Maybe it was my clothes that kept me out of their social circles. Didn't any of them wear stuff from the thrift shop?

I went home and found the last edition of the *Vineyard Gazette*, a properly famous newspaper that deals only with island issues. If World War III ever breaks out, it won't be mentioned in the *Gazette* unless some Vineyarder is involved.

I sought and found the paper's social columns and noted the names of the people who wrote them. Then I drove to Daggett Street and got in line for the little three-car On Time ferry, because Norton's Point Beach was closed.

During many weeks of the summer tourist season, the ferry is the only link to Chappaquiddick because the Wildlife and Fisheries people close Norton's Point Beach, the only other way to get there, to SUV travel, in their continuing failing effort to thus safeguard plover chicks until they can fledge. Few do, since plover eggs and baby plovers are favored meals for natural predators, but the Fish and Wildlife people can't close the beach to the gulls and skunks, so they close it to SUVs instead. Our tax dollars at work. No wonder Ethan Bradford lived in the woods and tried to ignore the last century.

It was still pretty early in the morning, so the ferry line wasn't too long, consisting as it did of fishermen hoping to nail bluefish along East Beach and workmen going over to construct houses such as Ron Pierson's castle-in-progress.

I was heartened, not for the first time, by the innocence of the earth and its people: even as war, pestilence, and plague slew thousands, normal life for most people continued. Farmers toiled in their fields, children played, artists painted, and women continued that work that is never done. The carpenters and fishermen who were going to Chappy that morning had not stopped their lives because two men had been murdered there. I, on the other hand, was going there because of the murders.

There is a single Z-shaped paved road on Chappy. It leads from the ferry to the sandy entrance of Dyke Road, then zigs to the right, where it becomes Chappaquiddick Road before zagging to the left, where it becomes Pocha Road. The pavement ends rather arbitrarily before Pocha Road does, and first-time Chappy bicyclists are often unpleasantly surprised to discover that they have to pedal a long way on sand and dirt before they get to Wasque Beach on the south shore.

Dyke Bridge, still the Vineyard's most popular tourist sight half a lifetime after the accident that made it famous, is at the end of Dyke Road, and is usually an objective of my Chappy trips since it provides the only access to the far beaches that constitute my favorite part of Martha's Vineyard. Today, however, I wasn't going fishing, I was going to visit Maud Mayhew. So I followed the paved road until I got to the postal box that marked the end of her driveway. The sign on the mailbox announced that I had come to Black Duck Farm.

Black Duck Farm lay between Chappaquiddick Road and Pocha Pond. It had been there a long time and had once provided a livelihood for its owners. Now, however, it was like most farms on the Vineyard, large acreage still under partial cultivation, but one supported by its owners rather than the other way around. Poor people didn't own farms on Martha's Vineyard anymore; they had been replaced, mostly by gentlemen farmers. Or, in this case, a gentlewoman farmer. Not that

Maud Mayhew could be considered gentle in any sense other than her pedigree.

Her long driveway took me past fields and through trees until it formed a loop in front of the spacious farmhouse that was her home. Barns, corrals, and outbuildings were across the loop from the house. They, like the house, were old but well maintained. A John Deere tractor and an ancient truck were parked beside the barn, and Maud's pickup was parked in front of its wide sliding front doors. Beyond the barn I could see cattle sharing a pasture with horses.

I parked in front of the house and knocked on Maud's front door. Nothing happened, so I walked around to the kitchen door and knocked again. This time Maud answered. Her eyes were red, and she looked older than when I'd seen her at my house, and when she spoke her voice was dull.

"What brings you here, J.W.?"

"I'm here because I'm sorry about Harold. You asked me to look after him but now it's too late. I feel to blame, somehow. I wish things were different."

She studied me then shook her head. "You had nothing to do with Harold's death."

"You may be right, but I'm going to try to find out who did it and why. I know it's too late to help him, but I want to do this, at least."

"The police say they'll find out who and why." Her voice was without emotion, and sounded like it came from a tomb.

"Probably. But I'm going to try, too. I wanted you to know, and I wanted to tell you that I'm sorry about your son."

"You have nothing to be sorry about," she said. "Thanks for coming. Now go home to your family." She stepped back and shut the door.

I listened to her slow footsteps as she moved away into the house. I had questions to ask her but couldn't bring myself to knock on her door again.

I went back to the Land Cruiser and looked around the yard, wondering where Harold had fallen. There was no police tape in sight, but the location of Maud's pickup suggested that the barn also served as a garage. I walked to the barn and slid back one of the large doors.

Inside was a blue, middle-aged Jeep Cherokee with underinflated tires. Those tires allowed it to drive over sand. My tires were like that, as were the tires of many a fisherman's truck. I memorized the Jeep's

81

license plate number, and wondered if whoever had killed Harold had been hiding in here waiting for him to come home.

Harold's body, according to the newspaper account, had been found out in the driveway. Even if his attacker had waited for him here, he had apparently killed Harold outside the building.

Unless he had dragged the body out there after the killing or Harold had managed to get that far before he died.

Had Harold known and trusted his attacker enough to let his guard down, or had he not seen him or heard him until it was too late? I wondered if Harold had any defensive cuts or bruises on his arms or hands.

Many people, police and others, had been in the barn since the killing, so I'd find nothing there that hadn't already been found, but I walked through the building anyway, taking note of doors and windows and hiding spots for assassins. I went out through an unlocked back door and circumnavigated the building before returning to my truck. I saw no indication that Maud had noted my snooping. Perhaps if she had, she just didn't care. I walked around the circular drive and looked at the ground. There were tracks of many cars, including police cars, no doubt. Too many for me to learn anything.

Whoever had killed Harold had either walked into the farmyard or had driven there. If he'd walked in, he either lived nearby or he'd parked his car somewhere before taking his hike. If he'd parked his car somewhere, some eagle-eyed Chappy person might have seen it and remembered it.

If he'd driven in, he'd have had to have parked his car somewhere. If he'd planned to ambush Harold, he'd probably have hidden it. The best place for that was behind the barn, but I'd seen no car tracks there. If he'd parked it in plain sight, Harold would have seen it when he came home.

Maybe he didn't care if Harold saw him.

How had he known that Maud wouldn't be there that evening?

Would he have killed her, too, if she were?

I thought about the island's old families. A lot of people in this case seemed to be members of one or the other of them. Was there a tie-in, or was I just spinning webs for nonexistent bugs? After all, only the Mayhews and Ron Pierson were undeniably involved, and both were victims. The other families — the Bradfords and the Peases — were only in the mix because I'd put them there. Or were they?

I was sailing on a sea of ignorance in a boat that was full of holes. I didn't know where I was going and I had no real business leaving shore.

I got into the Land Cruiser and drove back to the ferry landing. Not many Chappy people wanted to cross over to the other side, so I had only a short wait. When the captain of the ferry came by for my ticket, I asked him if Harold Hobbes drove a blue Cherokee. Yes, he did. Too bad about poor old Harold, he added. He hadn't been a bad guy, really. A little strange, maybe, but not a bad guy.

I looked somber and agreed. When I left the ferry I drove into town and found a parking place on School Street. I had an hour before the ever-vigilant meter maids and men would attach a ticket to my truck. I used it to go into the library of the Historical Society. Ed was there.

"I thought you guys were supposed to be moving this operation to West Tisbury," I said. "You don't look like you've made much progress."

"We'll get there," said Ed, who was the society's expert on logbooks from whaling days. "When we do, we'll need some guys with strong backs and weak minds to help us out. We'll call on you."

"Do that. Meanwhile, I want to read up on the island's old families. You have any suggestions about where to start?"

"I don't think you should plan on passing yourself off as a long-lost son at this late date," said Ed, "but come with me. I'm sure Arthur can steer you to some sources."

And he was right. Arthur could and did.

7

Banks's three-volume *History of Martha's Vineyard* is the place to start looking for information about the island before 1911. I had a set of the books at home but worked on the Historical Society's copies for a while. As is typical when I do research, I mostly encountered information having nothing to do with my interests. I am also typically distracted by such discoveries, which is not good for my detecting. Proper sleuths, unlike me, stay focused on what they're doing.

I read once more how in 1695, when Nantucket separated itself from the other islands then composing Dukes County, the existence of a single word in the legislation officially, if accidentally, transformed "Dukes County" into "the County of Dukes County," a curious name at best but one which, three hundred years later, still boldly identifies such institutions as the County of Dukes County Airport and the

County of Dukes County Courthouse, and gives citizens of the county a certain amused pride.

I learned that Sengekontacket Pond originally had been Sanchacantocket Pond, that Wasque had originally been Wannasque, and that Cape Higgen and Cape Pogue are corruptions of other Wampanoag names that have nothing to do with capes.

In Volume III, I spent some time on genealogies, but only reaffirmed what I already knew about the Mayhews, Bradfords, Hobbeses, and Peases: that they were old island family names, and that members of the families had from time to time married members of the other families.

This triggered a memory of my father's long-ago observation that during the winter when the tourists were gone, islanders played Monopoly with real properties and traded spouses so often that everybody on the Vineyard was related to everybody else

In truth, at one time there was so much intermarriage, and rumored incest up-island, that deafness was commonplace among Vineyarders and many of them used a kind of sign language without giving it much thought. Improved transportation and a growing influx of new blood put an end to the deafness, but not before it attracted scholarly interest from university professors who visited the island and published their findings in learned journals.

I wondered if any of this generation of Mayhews, Bradfords, et al. suffered from congenital deafness. If so, I hadn't noticed it. But then how would I, since the only one I'd ever talked to was Maud Mayhew?

I turned to other sources and read accounts of land dealings, disputes, business arrangements, whaling ventures, religious activities, balls, marriages, divorces, the establishment of educational institutions, and other island activities involving both the old families and newer ones.

Out of this came little information of use to me other than the general truth that old families were not necessarily richer or more morally upstanding than any others. There were good, bad, and indifferent Peases and Hobbeses and Bradfords and Mayhews. There were failures and successes among all of the families; there were scholars and fools; there were ministers and sinners (some of whom were one and the same); there were paupers and millionaires and middle-class citizens. The old families, in short, were mostly much like the newer ones.

Mostly, but not entirely. Some of their wealthier factions socialized together rather than with newer arrivals. They married, divorced, and had affairs with one another more than with those outside their circle. Similarly, they feuded and sued and fought with one another more than they did with younger island blood.

Some battled like the Campbells and the MacDonalds while others loved like Damon, Musidora, and Pythias. For better or for worse, these families' lives had been entwined in complex and elusive ways for over three hundred years. And still were, apparently.

Ed came by with an ancient logbook under his arm. He peered at my pile of books. "Ah," he said, "is this scholarship linked to the death of Harold Hobbes by any chance?"

Smart Ed. "Sort of," I admitted.

"Memorial services for two murder victims in a single week," said Ed. "They're planting Ollie Mattes later this morning and I hear they'll do the same for Harold on Saturday. It should be interesting to see who shows up for the church services. Do you think the causes of death will increase the crowds?"

This morning, eh? I looked at my watch.

"Excuse me," I said, shoving my books aside and scrambling to my feet. I ran out of the building feeling Ed's widened eyes on my back and got to my truck just in time to escape a ticket from a young meter man wearing an Edgartown summer cop uniform. He took his failure to increase the town's income with good grace, and even wished me a happy day as I pulled out of my parking place.

At home I made a couple of phone calls and learned that services for Ollie Mattes were to be held at St. Elizabeth's. Should I have been surprised just because Ollie had been at least as irreligious as I am? Probably not, since churches specialize in dealing with sinners, and Ollie was therefore probably more than qualified for St. Elizabeth's attention as he passed on to wherever it is that dead souls go.

Zee wisely opted not to attend services for someone she really didn't know, and I vetoed Joshua's and Diana's votes to go.

"We'd like to go, Pa. We've never been to a funeral."

"No. There's just a lot of talk and prayers and then they take the coffin to the

90

graveyard and there's more talk and prayers. There's not much to see."

"We'd like to go anyway, Pa."

"No. And don't tell me that all of your friends get to go to funerals."

"Aw, Pa. We never get to do anything."

I pointed at the sign above the kitchen door. "What's that sign say?"

"It says, NO SNIVELING."

"You know what that means."

Big sighs. "Yes, Pa."

"Good."

"Pa?"

"What?"

"Can we go next time?"

"Probably not. You can go to all the funerals you like when you grow up."

"Pa?"

"What?"

"When are we going to get our computer?"

It was a lovely day for a funeral. The summer sun was warm and the blue arch of the sky curled high above human heads. I sat in the back row of the church's pews and looked at the people who attended Ollie's last rites. There weren't many of them, but Father Joe treated them to a more dignified service than Ollie probably deserved. Afterward I stayed where I was

91

and watched until the last person went out onto Main Street. I was pretty sure who Ollie's wife and kids were, since they had been down in front, nearest the casket. They looked solemn but not heartbroken. I was more interested in some other mourners.

I followed the hearse to the graveyard, then stood by my truck, well back from the grave, while Father Joe said last words over the late lamented Ollie. There was something primeval about the ceremony and I had little doubt that this rite of passage, in one form or another, had been of unparalleled importance since the dawn of civilization. And why not, for what greater mysteries are there than life and death? Whence came we? Whither do we go?

My take on it didn't involve souls or heaven and hell. Rather, my theory was that there is a constant amount of energy in the universe and that one of its forms is life. When that life ends, the energy takes a new form. The body's movement and heat cease. The corpse rots. A flower grows. A bee sucks its nectar. A bear eats the bee's honey and perhaps the bee itself. The bear dies and is eaten by worms. A tree grows in worm-rich soil; it's struck by lightning. Its energy takes the form of fire. Nothing is lost.

Today the energy that had been Ollie was being transformed. What shape would it take? Perhaps there was a God who knew. I doubted it.

When the graveside service ended I watched people walk back to their cars. Two of them, a man and a woman, spoke briefly to the widow and her children, then walked to a Volvo station wagon. The woman was Cheryl Bradford, and the man, who was about her age, had similar posture and facial bone structure. Brother Ethan, I guessed.

I got into my truck, and when the station wagon pulled out of the graveyard, I followed it. Cheryl Bradford drove up-island and took South Road to Chilmark, where she entered one of those narrow, sandy driveways that lead from the Vineyard's paved roads. The mailbox beside the driveway had no name on it, only a number. The Bradfords, like many of the Vineyard's moneyed families, preferred their privacy. Theirs was not the only large island house at the end of an inconspicuous driveway.

The more newly rich and sometimes the younger members of old families preferred to advertise their presence and display their success by erecting more observable castles. One such was the successful car dealer who had offended local sensibilities by building a hotel-sized house on Edgartown Harbor; another was Ron Pierson, who was in the process of doing the same thing on Chappaquiddick. Once, when the automobile dealer was asked what he'd do differently in light of the criticism he'd received for building such a giant structure, he replied with a wide smile that he'd build it bigger. So much for community sensitivities.

Bucolic Chilmark scorns wide roads and ignores the dangers their narrow, winding ones impose upon bicyclists, walkers, and moped riders, but I found a place to turn around without getting killed by traffic rounding blind corners and then found another place to park where I could see the Bradford driveway. I didn't have long to wait before a battered Jeep lurched out onto the road and turned toward West Tisbury. I had a good look at the driver's face as he checked oncoming traffic before pulling onto the highway. Ethan Bradford was at the wheel. I followed him.

He took a right toward Edgartown then a left on Old County Road until he came to another of those sandy lanes that are found all over the island. He turned into the narrow lane and I pulled over beside the road and waited a minute before following. The lane was winding and the Jeep wasn't in sight. Listing poles carried sagging wires parallel to the road. From time to time other narrow roads and wires split off the main one, causing me to slow and check tire tracks before going on. Fortunately for me the lane was little used, so the Jeep's track was not hard to follow.

There is a lot more undeveloped land on Martha's Vineyard than you might guess. You can see it from the air, but not from most roads. Much of it was open grazing land a hundred years ago, but in the century since tourism seriously began to replace agriculture as the island's chief economic base, the fields have become new forests crisscrossed with fallen stone walls. Back in the trees are the foundations of long-gone farm buildings and houses, holes that were once cellars, old wells, and other hints at past sites of human occupation.

Around a sharp turn, the road I was following ended in a small meadow holding a badly maintained house. Its roofline was irregular and shingles were missing from its walls. A rotting wooden fence surrounded a vegetable garden between the house and a weather-beaten barn. The Jeep was parked in front of the house and beside it, facing me, a double-barreled shotgun cradled in his arms, stood Ethan Bradford. He still wore his proper funeral clothes but he reminded me of a young William Devil Anse Hatfield eyeing a McCoy.

I pulled alongside his Jeep and got out. I heard Baroque violin music drifting out of the house behind him, but it didn't impress me as much as the shotgun.

He stared at me with narrow eyes. "Who the hell are you?"

"J. W. Jackson. Are you Ethan Bradford?"

"You been following me since the graveyard. What the hell you want?"

"You know how to use a rearview mirror."

"I know how to use a shotgun, too."

I felt a little tingle of fear. "I didn't come here for trouble," I said. "I came to talk."

He cocked the weapon. "I'm not in a talking mood. Get your ass off of my property."

"You don't need a gun to get rid of me," I said.

"I may not need it, but I've got it. Now git!"

I was angry as well as frightened. "If you point that thing at me, I can charge you with assault with a deadly weapon."

"Not if you're dead." He sneered but he didn't point the shotgun.

"What do you know about Ollie Mattes's death?"

His eyes widened then narrowed again. "Nothing. Ollie fell off a cliff."

"The police say he was murdered."

"The police don't know shit."

"They know murder when they see it. He didn't have many friends, but you and your sister were at his funeral. You —"

I stopped speaking as he lifted the shotgun. It still wasn't pointed at me, but his finger was on the trigger. His voice was thin and cold like a winter wind.

"He wasn't my friend. You can choose your friends but you can't choose your relatives. Now get the hell off of my land before I have an accident cleaning this gun!"

I didn't want to turn my back on him, but I did. I got into the Land Cruiser and turned it around and left. As I did I heard him shout, "And don't come back!"

8

I'd willed my hands to stop shaking by the time I got back out to the paved road. There, still feeling ice along my spine and thinking about Ethan Bradford's words, I turned and drove back to Cheryl Bradford's driveway in Chilmark. I turned in past the PRIVATE PROPERTY sign that adorned the entrance and followed the lane to the house and outbuildings.

The site was another old farmstead, but this one, unlike the one I'd just left, was well maintained. The buildings and fences were painted and the house was well roofed and shingled. Beyond the house, to the south, an open field fell away to marshland that bordered a pond separated from the sea by a barrier beach. On the far side of the beach the waves of the blue Atlantic broke upon the sand. If you sailed straight south you'd see no other land until you fetched the Bahamas.

Once that field had probably grazed sheep or cattle, but now it held three horses. I remembered that Annie Pease had once taken a fall from a horse and that Uncle Ethan had been with her at the time. There are a lot of horse people on the Vineyard, but I am not one of them. Horses and I do not have a symbiotic relationship. When I ride one it's an uncomfortable experience for both of us, and we are mutually glad to bid each other goodbye as soon as possible. I wondered if my children, having failed to persuade me to get a dog, would ever make a plea for a horse. If so, they were doomed to further disappointment.

A horse trailer hooked to a sturdy SUV stood beside a large barn and corral. A tall red stallion was tied to a fence beside the trailer, saddled and ready to go. Cheryl Bradford's station wagon was parked in front of the house. I parked beside it and got out. I glanced at the horse and saw its head come up and its ears lie back as it stared back at me. It stomped a hoof and shook its beautiful satanic head.

"Don't worry," I said to it. "I'm not coming any closer."

I went to the front door. Cheryl Bradford herself answered my knock almost immediately and arched a quizzical brow over a polite smile when she saw me. She was still wearing her funeral clothes. Her sad eyes flicked over me from toe to crown. They were eyes you could fall into. Her smile was purely formal.

"Hello," she said, "may I help you?"

"My name's Jackson," I said. "I was at Ollie Mattes's funeral earlier, and I just came from your brother's place. He didn't seem to be in a mood to talk, so I came here. I hope I'm not intruding."

From inside the house a woman's voice asked, "Who is it, Cheryl? One of your men?"

Cheryl turned her head and said, "No, Mother. It's a Mr. Jackson."

"What does he want?"

"I'm about to find out, Mother." Cheryl turned back to me. "My mother still thinks I'm sweet sixteen and need watching. Now, what were you saying?"

I wondered if her mother might be half right. I said, "I was saying your brother didn't want to talk to me so I came here."

"I'm afraid I don't understand, Mr. Jackson."

I pulled up one corner of my mouth and tried to look a bit perplexed myself. "I'm sure you don't, Mrs. Bradford. It's just that

I have an interest in Ollie's death. My young daughter saw him fall down that bluff under Ron Pierson's house, you know."

Her maternal instinct kicked in as I'd hoped. "I didn't know. Dear me, I hope she wasn't traumatized. How old is she?"

"She's four, and she's fine. I don't think she even knows what she saw, in fact. We were sailing past the bluffs when it happened and the visibility wasn't too good. She didn't know it was a body. It wasn't until the next day, when I heard about Ollie, that I realized what she'd seen."

"I'm glad she's all right. But I'm afraid I still don't know why you're here."

I rubbed a hand through my hair. "I'll try to explain. It's like this. Ollie and I weren't best buddies or anything like that, but we used to talk. You know, about one thing or another. And we got along. Anyway, I feel bad about what happened, so I thought I'd tell somebody in the family about what my little girl saw and how Ollie had one friend, at least."

The reference to family evoked no response. "Why don't you talk with Helga?" she asked. "She was his wife."

I gave her what I hoped was an apologetic look. "She and the kids are grieving

101

right now, and I didn't feel right about interrupting. You know what I mean? But Ollie always spoke well of you and your brother, so I figured I would talk with one of you and you could tell them what I just told you. I hope I'm not putting you out by asking this. Maybe later, when Helga and the kids are more on an even keel, I can talk to her myself."

Her face maintained its small, polite smile. "We don't socialize a lot, but I'll be glad to tell her what you've said. I must admit that I'm a little surprised to hear that Ollie spoke well of Ethan. They didn't always get along."

I nodded my head. "Kinfolk don't, sometimes. But Ollie talked worse than he was. He put people off with his words, but they should have let it just roll off of them like I did."

"The way I heard it, he put people off because he promised to do landscaping for them and then didn't do it."

"Yeah, I guess there was that, too. Ollie wasn't a saint, but who is?" If I'd had a hat I'd have turned it in my hands about this time, but I had no hat so I touched my hair again and said, "Well, thanks for listening to me. Say, Ollie never told me exactly how he was related to you. Wasn't he a cousin or something like that?"

She studied me with thoughtful gray eyes, then said, "He was our half brother. Same father, different mothers."

"Oh," I said. "Well, that explains why he felt the way he did about you. Blood is thicker than water, like they say." I turned away and walked a few steps, then turned back. "Thanks again. I hope Ethan is feeling friendlier the next time we meet."

She had crossed her arms and her head was tipped slightly to one side as she looked at me. She was silent for a moment, then said, "Ethan isn't friendly to strangers very often. He likes to be left alone."

I gave her a crooked smile. "That shotgun of his will sure as the dickens keep me away from now on."

"He drove you away with a shotgun?" She looked faintly alarmed.

"Well, he didn't point it at me but he did say it might go off by accident. You might tell him that if he keeps acting like that he'll get himself into trouble. The next guy he threatens may go to the cops."

"You're not going to do that, are you?" Her voice was now full of concern. "He's been angry with the world since he left Connell Aerospace, but he's not violent. I know he can sound that way, but he's not.

He's my brother, and I know him. Please don't file a complaint. I'll have a talk with him."

"He worked for Connell Aerospace? Why was he angry when he left?"

"Because he was accused of stealing from the company and got fired. He came back to the island and he's been angry ever since. About what he calls modern times. He wants the world to go back to the way it used to be."

It was a common desire based on a fantasy about the Good Old Days, when things were uncomplicated and people were good and you didn't have to lock your doors at night. Earlier generations probably rued the loss of those simpler, better times when the king was wise and just and people were happy and there was no war or famine or pestilence. A lot of people on Martha's Vineyard were similarly nostalgic. To hear them talk you'd think that the hardscrabble life of earlier islanders, when the roads were dirt and money was scarce, took place in a paradise now lost, and that modern civilization with its noise and bustle was ruining everything.

I felt that way myself sometimes, although I knew my feelings were based on nonsense.

"What does Connell think your brother stole?" I asked.

"I'm not sure. They get a lot of military contracts. Maybe it was something he was working on. He says he didn't steal anything. I know he didn't like the way technology that could improve things was being used to make them worse. Ethan went to England once and when he came home he said that the museums were all filled with examples of human ingenuity devoted to war. He said the museum at Greenwich was the only one where there were no weapons on display.

"But he blames Ron Pierson personally for firing him. Pierson is CEO of Connell, you know. Ethan says it's just another example of the family feud between Ron's side of the family and ours. You should hear what my mother has to say about Ron. She hates every one of the Piersons, for that matter."

"Family fights can get pretty messy. Well, don't worry about me going to the police. But do have a talk with your brother before he gets himself into trouble."

"I will. Thank you."

"Did Connell ever find the gadget that went missing?"

"I have no idea," she said.

"I hate to think of the millions of dollars that get lost like that when the government does any kind of business. Makes you sorry you have to pay taxes."

"Ethan would agree with you about that." She looked up into my eyes. "Is there anything else you want to know, Mr. Jackson?"

She looked tired and sad, but she was an attractive woman. "No," I said. "But if I think of anything, can I contact you again?"

"Please do."

A lean, leathery, gray-haired woman appeared in the room behind her. She was wearing leather boots and jodhpurs and carried a hard hat in her hand. She could have been fifty or eighty. She looked at me with hooded eyes. "Oh," she said. "I didn't think you still had company, Cheryl."

"This is Mr. Jackson, Mother. He was just leaving. Mr. Jackson, this is my mother."

"Nice meeting you," I said. "I hope I haven't interrupted your riding plans. That's quite a horse. I don't think he likes me."

"He and I get along very well, Mr. Jackson. If you'll excuse me." She turned and left the room.

"My mother didn't like my husband," said Cheryl Bradford. "Since he died she still thinks I have poor taste in men."

"I'm sorry about your husband," I said.

"He's been dead for many years, but thank you."

We exchanged good-byes and I drove away, feeling her eyes follow me.

A woman named Eileen Graves wrote about Chilmark doings in a weekly newspaper column. She had been at it a long time and was one of several correspondents, mostly women, who kept islanders informed about the human-interest events in the various towns. She lived up by Beetlebung Corner, not too far from the Bradford farm. Since it was not yet noon I thought she might be home. I found her house and knocked on the door.

The woman who came to the door was gray-haired and had rounded lines. She wore what my sister Margarite calls sensible shoes and what was once widely known as a housedress and maybe still is. A pair of rimless glasses sat on her nose.

I introduced myself and asked if she was Eileen Graves. She admitted that she was.

"I'm doing some research on Vineyard families," I said. "I've been told that you're the person I should talk to about Chilmark people."

Flattery, some say, will get you nowhere. They're wrong.

"I keep my ear to the ground," she admitted with a smile.

"I won't intrude on you very long because I know it's almost lunchtime. What I need is a clarification about some relationships. I'm not so much interested in personalities as I am in genealogies. Who married who and who the children were and that sort of thing. They say you know more about that than anybody else in town."

"Small-town comings and goings are my subject, Mr. Jackson, not genealogies."

"I'm interested in the Bradford family. I've already talked with Cheryl Bradford, but I'm afraid I'm still unclear about some of the family relationships. Maybe you can straighten me out."

"Well, come inside and we'll see."

She led me into a sitting room and we sat across from one another in comfortable old overstuffed chairs with doilies on the arms.

"Now then, Mr. Jackson, let's see if I can help you."

"My friends call me J.W.," I said.

"All right, J.W. My friends call me Eileen. Now, how can I be of assistance?"

"For starters, let me tell you what I know. I know that Cheryl and Ethan Bradford are brother and sister. I also know that Ollie Mattes was a half brother of theirs who had the same father but a different mother. I know that Cheryl was married to George Pease and that she has a daughter named Annie. George Pease has been dead for some time. I take it that she hasn't remarried."

"You take it right. George got killed by a horse, you know. The Bradfords have always been horse people and they say he was trying to measure up by gentling a stallion the family owned. They found him in the stall and there was blood on the horse's shoes. Pretty traumatic. I believe young Annie fell off of a horse a while back and landed on some barbed wire. But they just stitched her up and sent her home."

I thought of the stallion I'd just seen and could easily understand how you might get hurt taming or riding one. I said, "What I don't know is who Cheryl and Ollie's father was, who their mothers were, whether there are more children or husbands or wives, and what their names are. It's all very confusing to me."

"Can I ask what you're planning to do with this information?"

"Sure. I'm thinking about getting my children a computer and it occurred to me that one of the things I might put on it is a short history of the island's old families. I've read Banks and I've seen some newer material at the Historical Society, but I can't find much about the last generation or two. I'm hoping you can tell me about the Bradfords, since they're Chilmark people. For instance, I had no idea until today that Ollie Mattes was a relative. Too bad about poor Ollie."

"I didn't know Ollie Mattes," said Eileen Graves. "I think he lived in Oak Bluffs, so he was out of my sphere. But I can tell you about Miles Bradford and his wife." She leaned forward and smiled wickedly. "And his other women, too, if that interests you. I love gossip!"

Who doesn't? "Tell me," I said.

9

"Miles Bradford was a man who liked his pleasures," said Eileen Graves, "and he didn't care where he found them. There used to be rumors around town that if sheep had last names, half the lambs in Chilmark would be named Bradford!"

I had to smile. "No."

"Yes! I think the sheep are an exaggeration, but there's no doubt he liked women and they liked him. I remember him well. He was tall and handsome and rich and randy. I think I have a photo of him in my files. Would you like to see it?"

"Sure."

She went away and came back with an ancient copy of the *Vineyard Gazette*. I looked at the face in the photo, which was part of an obituary notice. The face seemed familiar, but I knew I'd never met the man. "You won't find it in that obit," said Eileen, "but he died in bed with a

woman who wasn't his wife. Heart attack."
She arched a brow. "I imagine it was just
the way he would have wanted to go."

"The joy that kills," I said. "How'd that
story get out?"

"My husband was a doctor. He was
called to the house. In those days there
wasn't much going on in town that Jim
didn't know about. He kept his mouth shut
about most things, but he told me about
that. Now it doesn't make any difference
because Miles is long gone and so are the
woman and the child they produced."

"There was a child?"

"Miles fathered quite a few, some say.
This boy was Ollie Mattes, who just got
himself killed down in Edgartown. He was
Cheryl Bradford's half brother, as you
know."

"His mother was a Mattes?"

"She was still Alice Hobbes when she
and Miles were having their fling. She married Pete Mattes before the boy was born.
Pete gave the boy his name and treated
him like his own, but when Alice died Ollie
changed. He'd been a normal sort of kid,
but he got shiftless. When Pete died, he
ran Pete's landscaping business into the
ground. There's no telling why people
change like that, but Ollie did."

"He married a woman named Helga and they had children. Do you know her maiden name?"

She frowned and shook her head. "Girl didn't come from Chilmark. I can dig up her name but I don't know it offhand."

"I can find it if I need it. Did Miles's wife take exception to his affairs with other women?"

"It made a hater out of her, but she never made a public issue out of something she couldn't help. It was just that he had to have other women on the side. He was a man who needed more than one woman, just like there are women who need more than one man. I could name a few who are living in town right now, but I won't."

"Maybe I'll come back when they're dead."

She returned my smile. "Do that. I'm not inclined to slander the living, but the dead are fair game."

"I met Cheryl Bradford's mother earlier today. I didn't seem to please her."

"As I told you, Sarah's pretty sour on men, and after the way Miles acted up, who can blame her? She still lives there on the farm with Cheryl. Sarah is getting along in years and she's sick, but she's still tough as nails and strong as an ox."

113

"She looks stronger than she looks sick."

She nodded. "Brain tumor of some sort, I hear. Inoperable. When it kills her, it'll kill her quick. Until then she doesn't let it slow her down. Those Piersons are a rugged bunch."

"She was a Pierson?"

"Yes, indeed. The island branch of the family."

"What's her relation to Ron Pierson who's building that big house on Chappy?"

"Where Ollie Mattes was working when he got himself killed? Let me see now." She put her hand to her chin. "Ron must be Sarah's first cousin once removed. That would make him Cheryl's second cousin." She shut her eyes and sketched an invisible genealogy in the air with her forefinger. "Sarah's father's brother was Ron's grandfather. Yes, that's right. Those brothers never got along and Ron's grandfather ended up leaving the island." Her bright eyes opened again. "Family fights can be pretty brutal, as you may know. As far as I know, the younger generations are still at swords' points."

Love and hate are never far apart, and the memory of real or imagined slights can be very long. "What was the fight about?" I asked.

"Money, of course. Bill — that's Sarah's father — was the eldest, so he got the family farm that Sarah has now. Ben — that's Ron's grandfather — got the family swordfishing boat, which immediately sank, leaving Ben with nothing but a grudge. He turned a liability into success, though, and ended up richer than Bill by far. He moved to the mainland and got into the radio business — making them, that is. You've heard of Pierson radios, I imagine."

"No."

"Before your time, maybe. Anyway, Ben Pierson and Elmo Connell joined up making radios and other electronics, and when the space program was getting off the ground and the government needed communication systems for their rockets, Ben and Elmo created Connell Aerospace and began to get a lot of contracts. Ron Pierson isn't just his grandfather's heir; he's the CEO of the company. He's the richest Pierson of them all, and there are a lot of rich Piersons."

"And now he's back on the Vineyard building himself a house."

She nodded. "Yes, and a bigger one than any island Pierson ever owned. He's rubbing his cousins' noses in it, if you ask me."

"You think that's why he hired Ollie to work for him? To remind people that he's got the money now, and that his island kin have to work for him?"

"Could be. Ollie needed work, for sure, and he probably didn't care who paid him. I don't know Ron Pierson except for what I read in the papers. Maybe he's a prince among men."

I heard the irony in her voice. "Have you met many princes in your line of work?"

She shook her head and I liked her wry smile when she said, "No, princes are a pretty rare commodity these days. Always have been. Would you like a cup of tea?"

"I'd be glad to have one."

She rose and went out of the room. While she was gone I thought about what I'd learned. When she returned and we had tasted her tea — Earl Grey, as near as I could tell — I said, "Ethan Bradford worked for Connell Aerospace. But then he left the firm and moved back to the island. I met him earlier today and he was pretty unfriendly. Do you know anything about any of that?"

Her voice was as cool as her tea was warm. "What are you asking?"

I told her what Cheryl had told me about her brother. "I guess what I'm asking is how Ethan happened to go to work for a company owned by a branch of the family that was alienated from his branch. If the cousins were unfriendly, it seems curious that one would go to work for the other."

She shook her head. "I really don't know. Ollie Mattes went to work for Ron here on the island, remember. Maybe Ron's been making an effort to mend the rift in the family, but then again maybe that had nothing to do with it. Ethan Bradford is an electrical engineer, I know. He had the qualifications to work at Connell Aerospace, and if he applied for work there, maybe some sharp-eared middle-management guy recognized his name and gave him the job, thinking that was what the boss would want him to do. I don't know if Ron even knew he was employed there."

"Cheryl says Ron Pierson accused Ethan of theft and fired him and that it was personal."

She shrugged. "That could be the real story." She sipped her tea and then leaned toward me. "I'll tell you one thing, though. I don't like Ethan living out in the woods like Thoreau or one of those militia people you read about. It's not healthy for him and it's not good for the community."

"He's not living quite like Thoreau," I said. "He's got electricity and a telephone there in his shack. He's roughing it in comfort."

"I worry about what he might do."

"Do you think he's dangerous?"

"You saw him today. What do you think?"

An angry man with a shotgun is always a danger. "I'm not sure," I said. "His sister didn't describe him as a militiaman. As I told you, she said he was angry about technology being used for harm rather than for good, and about getting fired from Connell Aerospace. That doesn't sound like your typical antigovernment, rifle-toting hermit."

She looked at me over the rim of her teacup. "Maybe he's one of those militant pacifists who'll kill you for peace."

I thought of the radical animal rights people and Earth First! people and antiabortion people, and others of that ilk who were so full of righteousness that they considered it their moral duty to kill you if you acted against them. Passionate moralists have caused more grief in the world than all of its Darth Vaders combined.

"You may be right," I said. "For a small

island we seem to have a lot of oddball citizens. Did the Bradfords always produce their share? Some families do."

She laughed. "No more than the Jacksons, probably, but you'd know more about that family than I do."

"We're off-islanders, so we probably don't count," I said. I liked the way she laughed. She was a handsome woman who would have been a real looker when Miles Bradford had been in action. I wondered if Miles had ever made a pass at Dr. Graves's pretty young wife, but I decided not to ask. Instead, I said, "Aside from Ollie Mattes, did Miles father any other extracurricular offspring around the island?"

She finished her cup and placed it on the coffee table. "I'm not a census taker, but some say there are a lot of up-island people about your age who look something like Miles. His nose or hairline or chin or all of those and more. But Jim only told me about Alice and Ollie, because Miles died in her bed and not in someone else's."

Doctors, nurses, social workers, cops, and teachers know more about the Vineyard's dark side than most of its citizens and visitors can even guess at. Not all Snopeses live in Yoknapatawpha County and not all Beans live in Egypt, Maine.

The island has its share and more. The existence of a profligate wandering sex machine such as Miles Bradford seemed to have been was not a great surprise, and God, if there was a God, would not judge his children on the basis of which side of the sheets they were born on. Neither would I . . .

I put my cup beside hers and stood. "You've been a big help," I said. "From now on I'll make it a point to read your column."

"A new reader! What more could a writer ask?"

I thanked her at the door and she said I was welcome. I asked if I could call on her again if I thought of something she might help me with. She said I could. I got into my truck and drove home. One thing seemed clear: if Sarah Bradford was down on men, she had reason to be, considering the life her husband had led.

Happiness is having chowder in your fridge waiting to be heated. No one else was home so I prepared a large bowlful and feasted by myself, accompanying the hot chowder with a cold Sam Adams, America's finest bottled beer, although Sam may now hear hoofbeats close behind his horse as more and more small breweries enter the race. Whenever I think that America is doomed I remind myself of those eight hundred microbreweries and am reassured that the republic's future will be a glorious one.

When the chowder was gone and the cleaned dishes were in the draining rack I called Quinn at the *Boston Globe*. Quinn's lunch hours were irregular to say the least, but by a fluke he was at his desk. He and I had met years before when I was a rookie cop on the Boston PD and he was a young reporter. We'd hit it off for some reason and were still friends.

"I know what's happened," he said when he heard my voice. "Zee has finally wised up and left you and is on her way to my side. You want to prepare me for her arrival. You're a good fellow, J.W., in spite of what people say."

"You live in a rich fantasy world like all reporters," I said. "Didn't you write a story a few years back about Connell Aerospace? About how a small company making radios grew into a colossus getting contracts from NASA and the Pentagon? About cutting-edge electronics and weaponry and that sort of thing?"

"I did. You may be the only person who remembers it. Why do you ask?"

"You interviewed a number of people working for Connell, as I recall."

"And a number of their critics, too, as you may also recall."

"If you're still on speaking terms with any of your sources, I'd like to have you find out a couple of things about an engineer named Ethan Bradford."

"What kind of things?"

"He got through working there in the last year or two. I'd like to know as much as I can about what happened when he and Connell parted ways." I told him of my conversations with Cheryl Bradford and Eileen Graves.

"And why do you want to know this stuff, if I may ask before I go off and poke my nose where some people are sure to think it doesn't belong?"

"Because we've just had a couple of murders down here in Paradise and one of the victims was half brother to Ethan Bradford. I'm checking the family link."

"I read about those killings. And you're operating on the old 'people are usually murdered by relatives, friends, and acquaintances' theory, eh?"

"And the fact Ethan Bradford threatened me with a shotgun."

"Two reasons to be inquisitive," said

Quinn. "I'll see what I can find out. There may be a story in this for me."

"And while you're at it, try to find out if Ron Pierson, the company CEO, has any enemies mad enough to maybe try to burn down his house or kill his night watchman. Pierson owns the castle-in-progress where a guy named Ollie Mattes got himself whacked on the head and pushed off a cliff."

"I remember interviewing him for that last story, and I can tell you right now you don't get to be CEO of a major corporation without stepping on some toes."

"Try to find out if any of those toes belong to somebody who is really, really mad about it. There might be a fishing weekend here for you, in case you need more motivation than friendship."

"What a cynic you are," said Quinn, "to even imagine I'd refuse a request from an old pal. Now, what did you say your name was?"

10

According to Oak Bluffs town hall records, Helga Mattes's maiden name was Washburn. She and Ollie had married in OB. Their son Peter, born six months later, had been given the name of Ollie's stepfather. Helga was originally from off island, from out in Ohio, in fact. Apparently she'd been one of those girls who had come to the island for a summer of sun and fun and had ended up married to the man who had gotten her pregnant.

Or thought he had or was willing to think that he had or didn't care. There has always been so much free sex on the Vineyard that prostitutes have found it hard to make a living and girls are often unsure about just who fathered their children. In any case, Helga and Ollie and young Peter and his sibling had lived in a small house on East Chop while Ollie gradually destroyed the reputation of the landscaping business he'd inherited from old Peter and worked his way from relative economic comfort into poverty and finally into death.

It had taken him about a dozen years to manage that. I thought for a while and then went into the town clerk's office. The woman in the room smiled at me. "Can I help you?"

I gave her a small smile in return. Nothing too big, because I was on a serious mission. "My name is Jackson. I'm one of the investigators of the Chappaquiddick killings. I wonder if you can tell me where Helga Mattes is working."

The woman immediately became somber. "The funeral was this morning. I imagine you'll find her and the kids at home. I'm sure she's not working today."

I nodded. "Probably not. I'll need to speak with her sooner or later, but I don't want to intrude on her and the children right now. Meanwhile, though, I'd like to talk to her fellow workers. She may have told one of them something about her husband that would help our investigation."

"You're right to delay speaking to her today," she said, "but she's a friend of mine, so I'll be going by the house when I leave here." She leaned toward me and lowered her voice. "She works at the post office here in town, and she needs the job. Ollie hadn't been doing well lately."

I nodded again. "So I understand. Too bad about what happened."

Her eyes brightened. "Yes. Murder, they say."

"Homicide, at least."

"It's the same thing, isn't it?"

It isn't, but I didn't think there was any point in explaining the difference. I put sympathy into my voice. "How are she and the children handling the situation?"

She became confidential. "Just between you and me, I think they'll be fine. Ollie wasn't the best husband and father, if you know what I mean. Now, Helga will just have to support three people instead of four."

I didn't think I was the only person to whom she'd given that assessment.

"Sometimes a death is best for the survivors," I said. "I guess we should hope that's the case this time."

It was the woman's turn to nod. "I think it will be," she said. "I'm sure that Helga and the kids will be fine in the long run."

"Ollie Mattes apparently wasn't the easiest guy to get along with," I said, "but he didn't deserve to be killed. We're talking

126

with a lot of people who knew him, trying to get a lead on who might have done it."

Her confidential voice returned. "Yes. The Oak Bluffs police have been in here already. This place is a central station for town gossip and they wanted to know what we might have heard about people who were mad at Ollie. We passed on the stories we'd heard but of course we didn't really know if any of them were true."

"I doubt if you enjoyed naming names," I lied, suspecting that she actually enjoyed it very much. "It's not pleasant to suggest that people you know might be murderers."

"No indeed," she agreed, "but it is a murder investigation, after all, and we have to be of all possible help to the police."

"I appreciate your attitude," I said. "Duty isn't always enjoyable, but we have to do it."

"Absolutely."

"I'm working out of Edgartown and I haven't seen the Oak Bluffs report on what you folks told them. I'll head over to the station now and read it. Anything you think I should pay special attention to?"

She looked around the room as though there were someone there besides the two of us, then nodded. "You'll read about it anyway, so I can tell you that just before Ollie Mattes got killed, he got his nose punched by John Lupien. Then he hit John with a shovel. Then John had Ollie on the ground and was choking him before Helga broke up the fight, and I guess John threatened to finish the job if Ollie didn't mend his ways."

"What started it?"

She smiled and arched a brow. "You can probably figure it out. John works at the PO with Helga. He's single and she was in a bad marriage." She waggled her fingers as if the gesture explained all that needed to be explained.

"What ways did he want Ollie to mend?"

"Lately Ollie was getting rough with Helga and the children. He pushed them around, and when he slapped Helga and John saw the mark on her cheek, John went right after Ollie."

Another knight in shining armor defending another fair maiden from another dragon. Romance was not dead on Martha's Vineyard.

"Where'd you get the story?" I asked.

"The grapevine. I think John told somebody who told somebody."

"Ah," I said, nodding.

She nodded back.

I thought that if our conversation lasted much longer we were in danger of nodding our heads right off our necks, so I thanked her and left.

The Oak Bluffs Post Office is located between Circuit Avenue and Kennebec Avenue. I went there and was told by a man behind the counter that John Lupien had taken the day off so he could attend a funeral.

"I'm investigating the Chappaquiddick deaths," I said. "I understand that John and Ollie Mattes mixed it up a few days before Ollie was killed."

"You have a badge?"

"Sure." I put a hand on my back pocket then said, "Damn! It's in my jacket and my jacket's in the car."

"When you find it, maybe we'll talk." He gave me an unfriendly look and gestured to a man standing behind me. "Next."

Sometimes a fake works and sometimes it doesn't. I left and went down the street to the Fireside. The place wasn't crowded and I found a booth. Bonzo spotted me and came right over, a smile on his innocent face. Once Bonzo had been a promising young man, but bad acid had made him a child again. Now he pushed a broom at the Fireside and took orders for beer.

"J.W., how ya doin'? You haven't been in for a while. I know why, too. It's because you're married to Zee and have a family of your own, just like my mom."

His mother had taught school on the island forever, and Bonzo was and always would be her baby boy.

"You're right, Bonzo. How about bringing me a Sam Adams. And one for yourself, too, if that's okay with your boss."

His angel face immediately became sober. "Oh, no, J.W., I can't drink while I'm on the job. Sometimes I have one after work, but not on my shift. It wouldn't be professional."

"I guess you're right, Bonzo. My mistake."

He was happy again and brought me my beer. I sipped it. Just right.

Bonzo's ears are still good and bars are full of talk, so I said, "What's the latest news, Bonzo?"

Bonzo's dim eyes lit up as much as they could. "I guess you didn't hear, J.W. Last night some people were having a big party over on East Chop and all of a sudden the sound system just stopped working. The guy who's renting the house came in today and, boy, was he mad when he told us about it. He says his whole system has been cooked. He says the Silencer must have did it. He says he'll shoot him if he catches him. He says that sound system cost him thousands of dollars. I bet it might have, too, J.W. I looked in a catalog once and those speakers and everything cost a lot of money!"

"Exciting times, Bonzo. The Silencer strikes again."

"Say, J.W., you're pretty smart, who do you think that Silencer is, anyway? And how does he cook those sound systems? I mean, they say he cooks 'em in cars and in houses all the same. You play loud music and all of a sudden he'll cook your speakers. How does he do that? And how come he does it? He must not like music or something, don't you think? Or do you think maybe it's just the loudness he hates?"

"The smart money is on the loudness," I said, "but I don't know the answers to any of those things, Bonzo. It's a real mystery."

Bonzo nodded. "A mystery. Yeah, that's what it is, all right. Say, J.W."

"What?"

"There's bluefish around. You want to go fishing?"

Bonzo had neither boat nor car, so when he went fishing he usually went with somebody else and the somebody was some-times me. He was a dedicated and tireless fisherman who would cast all day and never be discouraged if he never caught anything or even got a hit. If he did catch something, he was filled with happiness and would take his fish home, where his mother would cook it and they would both enjoy a feast.

"That's a good idea, Bonzo. Say, why don't you come with me? I'd like that. When's your day off?"

"I got Sunday off. I can go with you right after church. That'd be good, J.W."

"I'll pick you up at your place after lunch. We'll have fun."

He beamed. "Yeah, we'll have a very good time. Catching fish is always a lot of fun. We'll see birds, too, I bet."

Birds and birdsong were his other pas-sions.

"We probably will."

"Well, I got to get back to work."

"Don't forget Sunday."

"Oh, no. I won't forget that!"

He went away and I drank my beer and thought about the Silencer. I wanted to know who killed Ollie Mattes and Harold Hobbes, but I didn't care who was killing the sound systems that too often filled the island air with head-pounding noise which was so bad that even Bach sounded wonderful by comparison.

Thoughts of the Silencer took me to thoughts of Mickey Gomes and the leaky jail in Edgartown and of Duane Miller, the gourmet jailbird. As usual in the law-and-order game, comedy and tragedy walked hand in hand down the mean streets.

And then I was thinking about my promise to the kids to get a computer. I looked at my watch and decided I had just enough time to begin trying to find out something about them. I finished my beer, went out to the truck, and drove to the computer store at the airport. They should be able to give me some advice. I hoped it wouldn't consist solely of recommending that I buy a machine from them.

11

The problem with talking to the guy at the computer store wasn't that he tried to sell me one of their computers or that he didn't know his business, it was that I had a hard time with the language he initially used to describe their wares.

He caught on to this pretty fast and changed to regular English. Apparently he was used to talking with computer-ignorant customers. "Maybe you should tell us what you want to do with your computer," he said. "Then we can put one together that will do that."

"All I know about computers is this," I said, ticking off my wisdom on the fingers of one hand. "You can use them as type-writers, you can use them to send and get e-mail, you can play games on them, you can look things up, like in an encyclopedia or in the library, and you can simulate flying an airplane. I don't know how to do any of those things but I know people who do."

"Computers will do a lot more than that," said the guy. "What do you plan to do with yours?"

"How about all but the games and the airplane? Or, wait a minute, can you play chess on a computer?"

"You can play chess or bridge or a hundred other games. You can play pinball."

"Really? You mean like a regular pinball machine? You flick the flickers and you can keep the ball in play?"

"Absolutely. You see the pinball machine on your screen and you flick the flickers by touching keys on your keyboard."

Nifty. But I didn't say that. Instead, I said, "My wife uses a computer at work and my kids use them at school. I'd need to get one that they can use."

"I'll tell you what," he said. "Why don't I give you some written material about computers? You can take it home and read it and talk about it with your family."

"That seems like a good idea."

"Two things you should consider are the speed of the computer — most people, including me, think faster is better — and the amount of information your machine can handle. Again, most people, including me, think the more the better, up to a point. You don't need to be able to store all the information the Pentagon stores, for instance."

"Probably not."

"One other thing you should know is that as soon as you've got your new computer it'll be out-of-date. A better one will be available the next day or maybe even later that same day." He smiled and shrugged. "It's a fast-moving technology."

"The newer the computer, the faster it is and the more information it can handle?"

"Yeah, that's usually the case."

"People already say I'm living in the past. You talk like I'm doomed to stay there because even though I have a computer it'll be out-of-date."

He grinned. "It's not as bad as that and we're all in the same boat. We get caught up when we buy new machines."

"How often does that happen?"

"Every three years or so, maybe. Something like that. Not everybody does that, of course. There's no reason to get a new one if your old one is still doing all the things you want it to. I know people who have computers that are ten years old or more."

I had a truck that was three times that old and I saw no need to get a newer one.

"Let me look at the written material," I said. "I want to see if I can understand the jargon."

He gave me some papers. "Maybe you should go down to the library and check out one of their *Computers for Idiots* books. They're meant for people like you who know nothing about the subject."

I looked through the pages he'd given me and saw words that meant nothing to me. "I think I'll take your advice," I said. I thanked him and drove to the Edgartown library.

The Edgartown library is on North Water Street, Edgartown's most prestigious thoroughfare, where summer parking is scarcer than chicken teeth. I found a spot up near the Harborview Hotel and walked back, passing the flower gardens and the great captains' houses.

To my left boats were moored in Edgartown's outer harbor, which lay between Chappaquiddick and the village. Sailboats were leaning into a southwestern wind as they came in for the night and momentarily shared the narrows with the On Time ferry. Tourists were on the sidewalk and in the street, ogling and photographing the sights. The walkers in the street reluctantly got out of the way of automobiles, because for tourists, it seems, Edgartown is such a make-believe place that they presume the cars are make-believe too and that the streets are really pedestrian walkways.

I went into the library and was greeted by Thelma Riggins in that friendly way all librarians seem to greet all arrivals. "Hello, J.W. What brings you into town in June? I thought you usually stayed up there in the woods until after Labor Day."

"I need a book on computers. One for complete ignoramuses who know nothing about them." I placed a hand upon my chest. "Like me."

"Heavens to Betsy, J.W., don't tell me you're thinking about getting a computer?"

"Shocking but true. I haven't decided yet, mind you."

She studied me. "Let me guess. The kids are both in school and they're on your back about this and Zee is on their side."

"It's worse than that. They've been after me for years to get a dog, but I won't have one in the house so now they've switched to a computer. I may have used up all my moral authority during my antidog campaign."

"Not that you ever had too much of that." She stood up. "I think I know just

138

what you need. Stay right there." She went away and came back and laid a book on the counter. "There you are. It's written in regular English and will tell you almost everything you need to know except what machine to buy, even though the new computers have bells and whistles that didn't exist when this book was written last year. You'll need some up-to-date writing to tell you about all that, but this will give you the basics."

"The book was written last year and it's already out-of-date?"

"Just like you and me, J.W." She laughed.

I was at the house reading the book when the kids came home from their last day of school. I expected many celebratory shouts, but they faded when Joshua looked over my shoulder. "Whatcha reading, Pa? Hey, look, Diana, it's a book about computers!"

Diana was so impressed that her mind was temporarily taken off both summer vacation and food. She, like her mother, could eat a horse and never get any bigger around the middle.

"Gee, Pa, are we really going to get a computer? That would be excellent!"

"I'm reading about them so I will have

some idea of what we need."

Joshua was already ahead of me. "Can we each have one of our own, Pa? Can we?"

Good grief. "Right now we'll have just one. You can both take turns using it for your schoolwork. Your mother and I will talk and then we'll all get together and decide what we need and what we can afford."

Diana thought fast. "Can we keep it in my room, Pa?"

Joshua frowned but before he could argue the point I said, "No. We'll keep it in the guest room. That will be the computer room, too. Now put your books away and get yourselves something to eat. I have a lot of reading to do."

"Okay, Pa. Pa?"

"What?"

"Can we get it today?"

"No. I have to study the subject and talk with your mother. She knows more about computers than I do. So do you, for that matter. I have to try to catch up. Now put your books away and get yourselves a snack."

"Okay, Pa. Pa?"

"What?"

"You're a good pa." Diana put her arms around me.

"Thanks, Diana. Now go put your books away."

When Zee came home I was deep into my book and fairly sure that there is truth to the notion that we learn faster when we're younger. She changed into shorts and one of my old shirts and made two martinis. Then she took me away from my reading up to the balcony, where we sat and looked out over our gardens, over Sengekontacket Pond and the barrier beach, now almost emptied of the cars that parked beside the highway there all day long, to Nantucket Sound, where the white hulls of boats were headed toward harbor.

We told each other about our days. When I finished telling about mine, she said, "You've been busy. Trying to decide what computer to buy must be relaxation after trying to remember who's related to who among the Bradfords and Ollie Mattes and all."

"Maybe if I had a computer I could keep a scorecard: who fathered who, who hates who, why who hates who, who loves who, who's whose sister or half brother, and so forth."

"You could at least do that. Maybe you can use it to figure when the fish will be hitting at Wasque. If you can do that you can be a rich man and you can retire."

I put my arm across her shoulders. "I have a working wife. Because of that, I already do so little work that nobody would be able to tell if I'm retired."

"There is that."

"You could retire, too. Do you want to retire?"

"No. I like being a nurse. For me the big difference would be that I'd be a rich nurse instead of just a regular nurse."

"There aren't too many rich nurses around these days. We could build a bigger house. One that doesn't have a leak in the northeast corner of the living room."

"I guess we could do that, although this house is just fine and that leak only leaks when there's a hard northeast rain. Besides, I know you'll be able to stop it one of these times. It can't get the best of you forever."

"It has so far. Maybe my computer will tell me how to fix it."

"True. Maybe it will tell you who the Silencer is."

"I hope not. I'm on the Silencer's side."

"Aiding and abetting a criminal is a crime, Jefferson."

"The music he's shutting down is the real crime."

"You crank Pavarotti up pretty loud when he sings 'Nessun Dorma.' "

"Apples and oranges." I emptied my glass. "We have to decide what computer to buy. Do you want to look at the reading material I brought home, or do you already have a good idea about what we should get?"

"I've been thinking about it all day, and I have some ideas, but I'll look at the stuff before we decide. We should talk with the kids, too, because they'll be using whatever machine we buy."

So we went downstairs and she and I studied the book I'd gotten from the library and the papers I'd gotten from the computer store. Then, after supper, we sat with the children in the living room and talked. Which is to say that I mostly listened while the other three talked, using words still new to me but familiar to them. When the talk was over, they seemed pleased and we all went to bed.

The next morning, which was Saturday, I made some early telephone calls to find out where Harold Hobbes's funeral was being held. But Ed had been misinformed. Harold was being cremated and Maud wanted no services. I didn't think Harold cared one way or the other, but I would

143

have been interested in seeing who came to the church and to the graveside.

But that wish was not going to be granted, so instead my family and I went to the computer store and bought a computer, a monitor, a printer, and a scanner and arranged to have a technician come to the house in the afternoon to set everything up and get us hooked up to whatever we needed to be hooked to. Then we went to the thrift shop and bought two two-drawer file cabinets.

At home again Zee and I rearranged the furniture in the guest room, then went out to the shed in back of the house and got an eight-by-two piece of one-inch plywood that I'd been saving since building the tree house in our big beech and that, by a miracle, was already painted. Deck Gray, a good traditional Vineyard color. We put the two file cabinets against one wall of the guest room and put the plywood across the two file cabinets and, lo, we had a desk to put the computer stuff on.

That evening I watched as first Zee and then the two kids clicked keys and pushed the mouse around. They played bits of games and experimented with playing music and motion pictures and entered and returned from the mysterious Internet.

Zee was careful, but Joshua and Diana were unafraid and seemed to remember everything they did.

Such was not the case with me when I was prevailed upon to take a turn. I forgot everything I thought I knew and was sure that I was going to destroy the machine if I hit the wrong key.

"Don't worry, Pa," said Diana, "if you make a mistake you just unmake it and go on."

She told me how to get onto the Internet.

"Now what do I do?"

"It's like a library, Pa," said Joshua. "You use your mouse to put your cursor right here and then you type in what you want to know."

I couldn't think of anything I wanted to know, but I knew I had to do something so I said, "How about opera?"

"That's good. Type in 'opera' and then click your mouse right here."

I typed and clicked and immediately my monitor screen informed me that it was listing the first ten of over eight million sites pertaining to opera. I couldn't imagine eight million sites pertaining to anything.

"What next?"

Diana knew. "Just click the first one, Pa. Put your cursor right here and click."

I clicked and found myself face-to-face with more information about opera than I knew existed. I read some of it.

"Okay, how do I get out of here?"

"Just click on that X up there in the corner, Pa."

I clicked and the page listing opera sites reappeared.

"Now what?"

"Click the X again."

I did and I was back where I'd started. The children gave me looks of congratulation. In exchange I gave up my chair to Joshua.

"You did very well," said Zee, patting my knee. "See, both you and the computer survived."

As I watched Joshua I decided that we'd done the right thing to buy the machine. Not only was I feeling better than I'd imagined I would, but my wife and children were happy and there seemed to be an almost unlimited amount of information available to us right there in our own house.

It was too bad that none of it had to do with the investigation I was making. I had bitten off a hard chaw and wasn't using my time well, as was clearly shown by the fact that although Harold Hobbes's murder was the subject of my inquiries, I'd somehow learned more about the Bradfords, the Piersons, and Ollie Mattes.

It was time to get back to Harold. I wondered where he had been the night that Ollie had died. He wouldn't tell his mother, even though he'd been afraid he might be accused of killing Ollie. I thought of the long black veil and of the man who'd been hung for murder rather than admit to having been in the arms of his best friend's wife at the time of the killing. Had Harold been in someone's arms that night? Was he so foolish or noble that, like the guy in the song, he'd die rather than reveal her name? And how about the best friend's wife? She hadn't said a word when they hung her lover.

Was there a link between Harold's mysterious night journey and his death? I watched as Joshua gave his chair to his little sister and thought how nice it would be if I could go on the Internet and type "Harold Hobbes's murder" and learn where he'd been that night, who had killed him, and why.

My computer couldn't tell me that, but some human could.

12

During the summer there are over one hundred thousand people on Martha's Vineyard. Of these, fifteen thousand, more or less, are year-round residents, which is about the same number as in a medium-sized town. As is the case in most such towns, the island's citizenry is a collection of different social groups, many of which know little about the others. On the Vineyard the separateness of these groups is emphasized by the fact that the island consists of six different townships, among which there are historical conflicts and ancient animosities. There are ten different police forces, six different fire departments, and a half dozen school systems, town offices, and highway departments. The regional high school, which was only built after decades of argument, is still the subject of passionate contention among citizens who favor it and those who think it never should have been built. The island also has groups of people who can be differentiated by vocation, avocation, interests, and proclivities.

Harold Hobbes had belonged to one or more of the various subdivisions of Vineyard society, the most obvious being that group of Chappaquiddick residents who, given their druthers, would have made a gated community of their peninsula. His mother, Maud, was chief among these defenders of Chappy turf, but she had already told me that she knew nothing of her late son's private life other than that he had had many women and his confession that he was the window breaker at Ron Pierson's mansion-in-progress. I'd have to go to some other guardian of Chappy to seek additional information about Harold's private life.

This plan posed two problems for me. First, the police, during the days since Harold's death, would almost certainly have already interviewed the Chappy people I might want to talk to and those people might see no good reason to talk to me, too. Second, even if the police hadn't talked to those people, they might not want to talk to me, since it was not a secret that I was in favor of open beaches on Chappaquiddick and everywhere else on the Vineyard. This was one of my two public postures in a life otherwise devoted to staying out of arguments, the other being opposition to the closing of open land to traditional uses such as hunting, hiking, and picnicking, and it was probably enough to get me viewed by the Chappy privatizers as an enemy.

I would have to give some thought to how to infiltrate that fortress mentality, but meanwhile there were other people I could talk to. One of them was Dennis Wilcox.

Dennis was a fisherman who worked out of Edgartown, usually with Silas Look as crew. His boat was the *Lucy Diamond*, a forty-footer he kept on a stake between the Yacht Club and Reading Room dock, not far from where we kept the *Shirley J.* He had a string of conch traps and did party fishing during the derby. Now and then, just to keep his hand in, he'd mount a pulpit on the *Lucy*'s bow and go with a few friends down to the Dump, south of No Man's Land, looking for swordfish. He wasn't the best harpooner on the island because he didn't get much practice, but he wasn't bad, and I'd gotten many pounds of fresh swordfish from him over the years.

I went down to the docks early the next morning, to catch him before he went out, because traps need to be tended whether or not it's the Sabbath. I saw that he was already on his boat, so I got my dinghy and rowed out there. There wasn't much wind and the water was almost like glass.

Dennis looked down at me as I pulled alongside. "J.W., what brings you out here? You going sailing?"

"No, I wanted to see you."

"You want to go conching?"

"No. My mind is weak but it's not that weak. It's about Harold Hobbes."

He glanced at me curiously while he coiled a line. "What about him, aside from his being dead?" He looked toward shore. "You see Silas? He's supposed to be getting us coffee."

"I didn't go by the Dock Street."

"Probably gabbing with somebody there. We should have been under way by now."

Dennis hadn't bothered shaving that morning. He was a broad-shouldered young guy who could haul a trap better than most, and being a worker he was characteristically anxious to get moving.

"Did you know Harold?" I asked, moving my oars slightly to keep the dinghy steady on the flat water.

He looked back at me. "I knew who he was. Why?"

151

"Harold was off someplace the night Ollie Mattes got himself killed. He wouldn't tell his mother where. I wondered if you might know."

His voice changed. "Why should I know?"

"He was somewhere he didn't want to talk about. It occurred to me that he might have been in the closet. If he was, I thought you might know about it."

Dennis had stopped coiling his line. Now he completed the job. "The island is a small world, but I can't claim to know everybody in it."

"Did you know Harold?"

He looked toward shore. "There's Silas, finally. Come on, Silas, we're losing half a day!" His eyes came back. "No. Only that he was one of those letters-to-the-editors writers who are always bitching about overdevelopment and golf courses and like that. I doubt if I ever said two words to him."

"You ever hear about him living the life?"

"No. Doesn't mean he wasn't, though. I don't subscribe to a dating service, y'know."

I said, "I'm not trying to corner you, Dennis. It's just that two men are dead and

I'm trying to find out where Harold was the night Ollie was killed. Somebody knows and I'd like to talk with him."

He finally let his anger show. "You think we've got one of those gay killers on the loose? Is that it? Well, all I can tell you is that I've never heard any of my crowd mention Harold Hobbes's name except when they read his letters in the papers and said they thought he was another one of those rich guys who never had to work for a living and didn't know shit from sardines." He turned and shouted toward shore, "Come on, Silas, we're burning daylight!"

"Will you ask around and let me know if you hear anything?"

He took a deep breath. "Sure, J.W., but if there was anything to hear I think I'd have heard it by now." He turned away and touched a key and the deep growl of the *Lucy*'s engine rumbled in my ears.

As I rowed back toward Collins Beach, I watched Silas arrive at the *Lucy*, hand up a thermos of coffee, and climb aboard. As I rounded the Reading Room dock, Dennis and Silas were headed out to sea.

I drove back home and found that a line had formed at the computer. Zee, as senior member of the users, was in front of the monitor screen and seemed to be reading something about Mongolia, while our children anxiously waited their turns. Mongolia? I decided not to ask why. Instead, I went to the phone book and looked up Roger Avila's number. Roger wasn't home. I guessed where he might be and phoned Helga Mattes. No one was there, either.

I looked at my watch, which I'd gotten for a dollar at a yard sale. You should never pay more than $9.99 for a wristwatch, and you can usually get a good one for less. Expensive watches get lost and broken just as often as cheap ones. They don't keep time any better and you worry about them more. All you need is a watch that runs, that's water resistant, and that's fairly shock resistant. Most fit that description. According to mine, a lot of people were at this moment probably in church.

Since I obviously wasn't going to be missed by my family, I went into the bedroom and got my old Boston PD shield out of the box where I keep mostly unused items like cuff links, tiepins, my ancient and long unused Zippo lighter, and a little water pipe left over from my pot-smoking days. I put the shield in my wallet then drove to the cemetery where Ollie Mattes's new grave was still covered with flowers and greens. There were no mourners, so I drove to Helga Mattes's house, which was as devoid of life as was the cemetery. I parked across the street and waited.

After a while two cars came down the street. One pulled into the driveway and the other stopped in front of the house. Helga Mattes and the children I'd seen at the funeral got out of the car in the driveway. A man I remembered seeing at the funeral and grave service got out of the other car. He had stood apart from the widow and her children at the burial and had still been there when I'd left. The smart money said he was John Lupien. He and Helga and the children went into the house.

I was listening to the country-and-western station in Rhode Island. Some new singers whose names I'd mostly not heard before were singing unfamiliar somebody-done-somebody-wrong songs. Their bands were too loud for their voices so I missed a lot of the words, but it was music you could dance to, which I guessed was the point. Personally I preferred to hear the lyrics when I listened to C and W, but that seemed less fashionable now than when Emmylou and Dolly were at the top of the charts. I listened to two more songs and then crossed the street and knocked on the door. Helga Mattes opened it.

I said, "Mrs. Mattes? My name is Jackson. I'd like to offer my condolences to you. I was at the funeral."

"Oh," she said. "Thank you. Were you a friend of Ollie's?"

Did Ollie have friends? I said, "Not a close one, but no man is an island and one death diminishes us all."

"Yes."

"Yes. John Donne wrote it." I looked beyond her and saw a man watching me from the far side of the room. I dropped my eyes back down to hers. "I know this probably isn't a good time, but I'd like to talk with you about your husband. I'm one of the people investigating his death."

Her face seemed to stiffen. "Oh. Well, I've already talked with the police." She didn't ask me in.

"I know," I said, "but I'm interviewing people again on the chance that somebody might have remembered something they didn't mention before. Some name, maybe. Somebody who had reason to want to harm your husband."

"I've told the police everything. There are no other names that I can think of. Ollie didn't have many friends, but I can't think of anyone who would want to kill him. Don't they think he might have been killed by mistake? By someone who went there to burn down that big house or something and who fought with Ollie then panicked and pushed him off of that cliff to make it look like an accident and then ran away?"

"Yes, it could have happened just like that. But maybe it didn't. Maybe somebody wanted him dead. That's what we're trying to find out."

"But who would want him dead? My husband wasn't easy to like, but I can't imagine anyone wanting that. We don't just kill people because we don't like them."

Some people do, of course. "Usually people have a reason or think they have," I said. "Planned killings usually involve money or sex or fear, but the motive can be almost anything. It can be a political assassination or it can be as simple as getting rid of somebody who's inconvenient, or it can be love."

Her eyes grew wary. "What do you mean?"

I made a small gesture. "It's a commonplace event. A lover kills a husband to get the wife. A wife kills a lover who threatens to tell her husband about their relationship. A husband kills his wife so he can marry his mistress. A mistress kills a wife so she can marry the husband. Whenever there's a killing, spouses and lovers are always prime suspects." I flicked my eyes at the man behind her, then brought them back down to hers again.

She hesitated, then stepped back and said, "I've told the police everything I know. You'd better go now."

She began to shut the door, but I put a hand on it. "I'd like to talk with Mr. Lupien before I leave."

"No. Not now. Please leave." She pushed on the door but my arm was stronger than hers.

I raised my voice. "Mr. Lupien, I'd like to speak with you for a few minutes."

He was there instantly. "Take your hand off of that door before I take it off for you!" He was a sturdy man about six feet tall, and his voice was hard and angry.

I said, "You have a temper, Mr. Lupien. You don't seem to be able to control it."

"You heard what I said. Take your hand away!"

I took my hand away. "You tried to strangle Ollie Mattes not long ago and now I find you here with his wife. I'd like to talk with you about that."

Helga Mattes put her hand on his arm. "Don't go out there, John. Just shut the door!"

But John came out and shut the door behind him. "Have you no decency? Helga and the children are still in mourning."

I ignored his outrage. "Where were you when Ollie Mattes was killed?"

The skin on his face seemed stretched to the breaking point. I almost expected it to split and reveal the bone beneath. I'd never seen anything like it. Then, when he heard my question, he suddenly relaxed.

"I can prove I wasn't on Chappaquiddick."

"Where were you?"

"Right here. Right in this house. Helga can testify to that." His voice changed tone. "I love Helga. She was getting a divorce, and we're going to get married."

"If she loves you, she's not a dependable witness. Women in love will swear their men were home in bed even when surveillance cameras and fingerprints and DNA evidence say they were killing somebody across town."

He was confident. "Then ask the children. They were here, too. And no one was in bed. We were watching television. We

159

knew Ollie was at work, so I came over for the evening."

"Did the children approve of that?"

"They knew about our plans. They want their mother to be happy."

Helga and John's mutual alibi looked hard to shake, especially if her children backed them up. I shifted gears.

"Did you know Harold Hobbes?"

"No. Are you accusing me of murdering him, now?"

"Did you?"

"No. I didn't even know the man. Besides, some of us, including me, were working late sorting mail when that happened and there are witnesses who can testify to that. You seem pretty anxious to make a murderer out of me, Jackson. I don't like it!"

"I don't blame you. I wouldn't like it either. Do you know if Ollie knew Harold?"

"I wouldn't know."

"Helga might. I'd like to ask her."

His anger came back. "You stay away from Helga, damn you!" His arms hung by his sides but his hands became fists.

"Take it easy, John. She can answer here or at the station." Then I softened that threat. "No one thinks she killed anyone and I have no reason to think you did, either. But if there have been two violent deaths, and if there was a link between the victims we need to know about it."

"Helga needs some peace and quiet, damn it!"

I spoke soothingly. "She probably does. I'll tell you what. I'll ask her the one question. If she says yes, I'll have to talk with her some more later and get the details. If she says no, that's the end of it."

He took a breath and his fists loosened back into hands. "All right. But then you leave. Agreed?"

"Agreed."

We went back to the house and I asked the question. Helga said that she'd never heard Ollie speak of Harold Hobbes except to sneer at his letters to the editor. I took that as a no, apologized for my intrusion, thanked them for their help, and drove home wondering if one or both of them were lying.

13

It wasn't even noon and I already felt like I'd put in a full day. And on the Sabbath, too, when I should have been resting. What must the Lord God of Hosts think of me?

At home Diana was at the computer and Joshua was reading some printed material that had come with it. Zee was in the kitchen making a smoked bluefish salad for lunch. I put my hands on her shoulders and reminded her about my fishing date with Bonzo.

"It's nice of you to take him," she said. "Bonzo loves to fish."

"How are things in Mongolia?"

She threw me a smile. "They haven't been so good since Genghis Khan stopped conquering the world. Ulaanbaatar has polluted air, it takes eleven hundred togrogs to buy one U.S. dollar, and the country suffers from dust storms, forest fires, drought, and zud."

"Oh, no! Not zud, too!"

"I'm afraid so."

"What's zud?"

"Those of us who speak Mongolian translate it into English as 'harsh winter conditions.' Also, the country's landlocked, so there are no boats. I think you should think again about taking your vacation there."

"You've convinced me. Why the interest in Mongolia?"

"What's the greatest movie ever made?"

"That's easy. *Citizen Kane*."

"Right. The other night I got to wondering if Charles Foster Kane got his name from Genghis Khan, so this morning I looked Genghis up and one thing led to another and I looked up Mongolia while I still had my turn at the wheel."

"I thought it was Kubla Khan who built Xanadu."

"Genghis, Kubla, whatever. You've seen one Khan you've seen them all. You know what I mean? Besides, Coleridge was tripping when he wrote that poem, so how much can you trust him?" She put down her wooden tools and turned to me. "How about a kiss?"

I gave her one and said, "Well?"

"Well, what?"

"Was Charles Foster Kane named after Genghis Khan?"

"Beats me. I know that Mongolia is just a hair smaller than Alaska, but I don't know if Citizen Kane got his name from Genghis. Maybe if you look up Orson Welles on our snappy new computer you can find out."

"Some things are probably best left unknown," I said, but she'd given me an idea.

"Call the kids to lunch," said Zee.

I did that and after we'd eaten I claimed a turn on the computer. Diana was kind enough to show me how to turn it on and Joshua directed me to the Internet. Before I could do more, I was interrupted by Oliver Underwood, who jumped up onto the desk and walked across the keyboard. Strange things immediately happened on the screen. I removed Oliver, but was filled with fear as I looked at what he had created.

"What do I do now?"

Diana laughed. "Cats like computers, Pa!"

"But look at the screen!"

"Don't worry," said Joshua. "We can fix it."

He did something with the mouse, and the cat mess went away. I was back on the

164

Internet. Whew. "Show me how you did that."

He did, and I hoped I'd remember what he'd done.

"Now," I said in my calmest voice, "if I want to find out about somebody, how do I do it?"

"There are lots of ways, Pa."

"What's the easiest?"

Joshua was a good teacher. "Use your mouse to move your little arrow to this place here and click."

My arrow went flying all around the screen, but I finally got it pointed at the right spot and clicked my mouse.

"That's good, Pa. Now just type in the person's name. Good. Now you can put your arrow over here on 'Search' and click again."

I clicked my mouse and found myself looking at a list of sites all claiming to have something to do with Ronald Pierson.

I got more instruction from my children on what to do next, and clicked the first site. Up came information about Ron. However, as I read it soon became clear that I was not reading about Ron the house builder but about his father, Ronald, Senior, who had served as CEO of Connell Aerospace and allied industries between the reigns of Benjamin Pierson and Ronald, Junior.

Ron, Senior, had done a good job with his companies and had left Ron, Junior, with a healthy and expanding business empire, according to the writer of the article, whose tone made me suspect that he was a writer hired by the company.

My professorial children showed me how to get out of the site I was in and into another one, this one having to do with Ron, Junior.

Ron, Junior, had been born in Connecticut, had been schooled at Exeter and Yale, had served as a navy pilot in the first Gulf war, flying off of the *Teddy Roosevelt*, had married Jeanette Washburn of Shaker Heights, Ohio, with whom he had produced three children, and attended the Episcopal church. Upon his father's retirement, he had, at age thirty-five, taken over the reins of Connell Aerospace and other family companies and had brought them, bloodied but unbowed, through the turn-of-the-century stock market crash. He was now in his forties, about my age but very much richer.

The site included photos of handsome Ron and his handsome family at home, other photos of Ron's gigantic industrial plants, and others of Ron at work with his managers and workers.

I didn't see any photo of Ethan Bradford.

A third site consisted of an article on political speculation in which Ron, Junior, was mentioned as a possible candidate for Congress or even the presidency. He was a moderate Republican, fairly conservative in his financial views but liberal in his social ideas. He and his family were blessed by good looks, and he was considered a tough but fair employer by the unions whose men and women worked his industries. To the pundits who were quoted in the article, Ron seemed like a comer to be watched.

A fourth site consisted of a statement made before the Joint Economic Committee by a scientist who had reported on weapons technologies, including some being developed by Connell Aerospace. I followed the report pretty well at first, but when I got to magnetically insulated linear oscillators, neutral particle beam sources, and the use of magneto cumulative generators as explosive-driven power supplies, I realized that the English I'd studied in college was poor preparation for understanding what I was reading. I abandoned the site without tears, wondering if Ron Pierson himself understood any of this stuff, or whether he depended on his scientists to grasp it. I guessed the latter.

A fifth site was a paean to Benjamin Pierson and to the industrial empire he had built, including Connell Aerospace. I was working my way through the history of Pierson's business successes when Diana tugged at my sleeve.

"Pa?"

"What?"

"It's my turn now. I've been waiting forever."

I looked at my watch. Good grief. Bonzo must be wondering what had happened to me.

"I'm sorry," I said. "I lost track of time. Tell me how to get out of here."

She did so. The kid was a whiz.

I stood up. "Sorry for being so long, sweetheart."

"That's okay, Pa. Thanks, Pa." She climbed up into Captain Kirk's chair and began issuing commands to the computer. It obeyed with alacrity, knowing it was no longer dealing with an oaf.

"Well, how'd it go?" asked Zee. "Did you learn anything useful? Or anything at all, for that matter?"

"Enough to ask a question before I go fishing." I found Ollie Mattes's phone number in the book and called his widow.

"I'm sorry to bother you again," I said, "but I'd like to know if you're related to Ronald Pierson's wife."

There was a short silence; then she said, "She's my cousin. How did you know that?"

"You were a Washburn and so was she, and you're both from Ohio. I'd been wondering how Ollie managed to land that job as watchman. Would I be right in thinking he got it because you suggested it to your cousin?" There was another silence, so I said, "It's very understandable if you did. Ollie needed a job and Ron Pierson needed a watchman." There was another silence, so I added, "We can find out by talking to your cousin."

"All right," she said. "I did ask Jeanette to ask Ron to help Ollie. Ollie was having a hard time finding work and we needed the money and he pressed me to get Jeanette to help. He said families had an obligation to help their kin. He yelled at me. It wasn't much of a favor from Ron's point of view but it meant a lot to us. Are you blaming me for Ollie's death? All I did was help him get a job that he needed."

169

"I'm not blaming you for anything," I said. "You tried to help your husband. You didn't know somebody would kill him while he was working."

"I'm glad you think that way. I was just trying to do him a favor."

"I'm sure you were." She had also been doing herself and John Lupien a favor. With Ollie at work, the two of them could be together. But I didn't say that. Instead, I apologized again for intruding into her life and hung up.

I looked at the tide chart on the fridge, then kissed Zee, took two rods from their hangers on the ceiling of the living room, went out and put them on the roof rack of the Land Cruiser, and drove to Oak Bluffs.

A half hour later Bonzo and I were on Daggett Street and I was pleased to find us third in the ferry line, which meant that we'd be on the first ferry across to Chappy. At this time of day, though, most people who were going to Chappy were already there. The line on the Chappy side of the gut was the long one, as many of those people were already coming back.

There was a theory among some SUV drivers that there was collusion between the owners of the On Time ferry and the Fish and Wildlife people who closed

Norton's Point Beach. It maintained that the On Time carried a lot more traffic when the beach was closed, and that a percentage of the increased take was fed to the F and W people. Look for the money, the theorists would say, nodding wisely to one another.

We drove to Dyke Road and followed it past the Japanese gardens and over the bridge onto East Beach. There we took a right and drove past parked SUVs and the families of sunbathers and swimmers, some of whom were now packing up to go home as the sun headed west. At the south end of the beach I parked among trucks belonging to people who were more interested in fishing than beaching.

I saw no fish under any of the trucks, but people were making their casts instead of standing around drinking coffee and talking, so I knew that someone had recently bent a rod. I got my rod and gave the other to Bonzo and we went down to the water to join the other hopefuls. Bonzo was in heaven. He didn't care if he actually caught anything, he just loved to fish. In this case he got to both fish and catch fish. Two hours later we had a dozen nice midsized blues in the fish box and I put my rod back on the rack.

171

"That's enough for me, Bonzo."

"How about maybe just one more cast?" he said, his big empty eyes shining and his happy mouth full of smiles.

"Sure."

And his cast was a good one. There was a swirl of white water as he reeled in and then his rod was bent and the line was singing as the fish fought a wonderful losing battle to stay wild and free. But all things eat and all things are eaten and it was that fish's turn to be devoured, just as it would be my turn one day. The fish leaped and battled, tossing spray and racing first to the left, then to the right, but all the time being reeled closer to the beach until, finally, it was thrashing on the sand. Bonzo put his foot on it, careful to avoid the knife-pointed fins, hooked his fingers through its gills, careful to avoid the needlelike teeth, and carried it up to the truck. I used my plug retriever to get the redheaded Roberts out of the fish's dangerous mouth, cut its throat, and added it, still writhing even in death, to the fish box.

I put Bonzo's rod in the rack. Bonzo was happy. "Gee, J.W., I think that was the most excellent fishing I ever had!"

Good old Bonzo.

I felt tired but renewed. Most of the beachgoers had long since returned home, so the ferry line from Chappy was shorter than it had been when we'd come over. At the Sengekontacket landing off the boulevard, we scaled the fish and rinsed them clean. At my house, behind our shed, we filleted them, then buried the carcasses in the garden to fertilize the veggies and flowers. I packaged half the fillets for Bonzo's mother and half for myself, then drove Bonzo and his catch back to his house in Oak Bluffs.

He stood at the front of his mother's flowered walk, his arms full of packaged fish. "Gee, J.W., we did real good! My mom will be proud of me! Maybe we can go again sometime!"

"We'll do it, Bonzo. Say hi to your mother."

I drove home thinking about the ferry lines and wondering if Ollie Mattes and Harold Hobbes would still be alive if the Fish and Wildlife people had closed Norton's Point Beach two weeks earlier.

14

I'd barely gotten seated at the breakfast table
the next day when my son spoke up.

"Hey, Pa!"

"What, Joshua?"

"There's this kids' summer school, sort
of, and it sounds neat. Can we go to it?"

"Yeah, Pa," Diana chimed in. "Can we?
All our friends are going. And we can use
our computer to help us study! Please!"

A child's "please" can be an annoying
but powerful word. I looked at Zee. "Do
you know anything about this?"

She handed me a piece of mail. "This
came a couple of days ago."

I opened the envelope and read. The ad-
vertised program seemed mostly to offer
nature studies, including guided walks
though the Felix Neck Wildlife Sanctuary
and to various beaches. A big adventure
would be a trip to Woods Hole to see what
the scientists were doing there.

"It's only for a couple of weeks," said Zee. "I told the kids that I'd talk about it with you, but your son, there, jumped the gun." She looked at my son, who smiled back at her, unashamed of his brashness.

"I see here that it starts tomorrow. That's not much warning."

"Please, Pa! It'll be lots of fun!"

I looked at Diana, who was wolfing down her breakfast between pleas. It was hard not to want my daughter to have fun.

"We'll learn stuff, too," said Joshua, arguing the other virtue of education.

I turned to Zee. "We'll have to sign them up today," I said.

"It'll just take a phone call," she replied, sipping her coffee. "I already talked with Mr. Timulty and told him we were interested. The bus will pick them up at the end of the driveway and bring them back home again, just like during regular school. If you approve, that is."

How was I supposed not to approve? Was I getting old and feebleminded? First the computer and now summer school. What would my family talk me into next?

"Fine," I said. "It sounds like a good thing!"

The kids exchanged big smiles and Zee gave me one just for myself. I felt good.

Being a father had its moments.

The next morning after the kids left for their first class and Zee headed to the hospital, I phoned Maud Mayhew. Her voice had no vibrancy in it. I told her I wanted to talk with her, and if she had wanted to say no, she lacked the energy to do so. I got a package of bluefish fillets from the fridge and drove to Chappaquiddick. It was another lovely day, and already the pale June People were headed to the beaches to work on their tans so that when they went back to their jobs, their colleagues would know they'd been someplace where there was sunshine.

When Maud met me at her door I gave her the package. "Here," I said. "I caught this guy yesterday afternoon. Give it to somebody else if you don't eat bluefish."

Her tired eyes seemed to brighten slightly. "I do eat bluefish, but I don't get it too often these days. You'd think that I'd catch my own and have it all the time, living close to the beach like I do, but the truth is I don't go fishing much anymore and neither do any of my friends. Come in and sit down while I stick this in the refrigerator."

I went in and looked around. People in certain financial and social circles don't *buy* furniture, they *have* furniture. If some child or grandchild buys a house, it's furnished with things from another family house, never with new stuff. Maud Mayhew's house was filled with such furniture: tables, Persian rugs, and comfortable old couches and chairs that had surely been purchased by some Mayhew long since turned to dust and forgotten. Everything was worn but so well made that it would last several more generations. None of them, of course, would be the descendants of Harold Hobbes.

Or was that indeed the case?

When Maud came back from the kitchen she was carrying two cups of coffee. She gave me one and we sat down in leather chairs with a low Chinese table between us. It looked to be the kind brought home from the Orient by whaling captains or merchants in the spice trade.

She looked at me with those fatigued eyes and said, "Now, what do you want to talk about, J.W.?"

"I want to ask you some questions about Harold," I said.

"I've already talked to the police. You should leave this business to them." She sipped her coffee.

"They won't tell me things I want to know."

She shrugged shoulders that seemed to have grown thinner in the past few days. "What do you want to know?"

"Was Harold married?"

She raised her head. "They never asked me that. No. He was single. He lived here with me."

"Had he ever been married?"

"Once. A long time ago. Both of them were very young. It didn't last long. Why do you ask?"

"Because I may need to talk with her. She may know something."

"When Beth left she never looked back. That was twenty years ago. She's remarried and has been living on the West Coast ever since. You'll be wasting your time talking to Beth."

"You're probably right, but I may want to talk with her anyway."

She shook her head, but got to her feet. "Wait here." She went out of the room and came back with a slip of paper, which she gave to me. On it was Beth Johnson's name and a California address.

"He never married again?"

"No. Once was enough, he said. I was married three times, and he said he was going to break the family tradition. He told me that more than once. Usually when he was drinking. He could be cruel."

"Did he have children?"

Her thin lips formed a fleeting, humorless smile. "None to speak of."

It was the punch line of an old joke about a bachelor father of bastards. "Did he have any at all?" I asked.

The smile left as fast as it had come. "No. I would have known. We have money and I'm sure the mother would have come looking for some of it, but no one ever did."

I hesitated. "I don't want to anger you by asking this, but did he prefer the company of men?"

But she wasn't offended. She shook her head almost bitterly. "No, Harold chased women, not men. If you want the truth, I think he'd have been better off if he'd been homosexual. All those women!" She looked at me and her eyes showed a spark of life. "You don't know how cruel women can be. Worse than any man I've ever known! They have claws like lions and the consciences of crows. Hate can build up in them until they explode."

"I'd like to talk with some of Harold's women. Maybe one of them can give me some useful information. Do you have some names you can give me?"

"Of Harold's women? Or should I say his sluts? Oh, yes, I can give you some names." Her voice grew rough and angry. "He bragged about them to me when he was drunk, you know. He waved them at me like red flags, like a torero inciting a bull to charge. He wanted me to attack him so he could hurt me more and do it with a clean conscience, but I wouldn't give him the chance. I'd leave him drunk and raving and go to my room and lock the door." She held the coffee cup with both hands, squeezing it between her palms, then slowly relaxed. "The next morning, late, he'd be sober and hungover and full of apologies and promises." She looked at me. "They say that there's truth in wine, but I've always hoped that wasn't so."

You never know what goes on in families behind closed doors.

"I think it's just an old saw," I lied. "Do you think he was with one of those women the night Ollie Mattes was killed?"

"No. If he'd been with one of his girl-friends he'd never have hesitated to use her as an alibi. He liked being known as a la-dies' man. He liked loving and leaving them. He wouldn't have hesitated to give the police her name."

"He wouldn't have been reluctant to

ruin her reputation?"

She gave me a look of sour amusement. "What century do you live in? These days love affairs don't ruin reputations. Women write books about their love lives. They hire publicists. Men are just as bad."

Some famous people flouted infidelity, of course, as did mistresses anxious to be famous, but I wasn't so sure most other people did.

I got the names of five women from Maud. Two of them lived on Chappy and the other three elsewhere on the Vineyard. I recognized only two of the names. Maud seemed to repent her earlier characterization of them as sluts. "I know the two who live here," she said. "They belong to CHOA, in fact. That's where Harold met them. They're just women with too much time on their hands. Some women like that think a fling will cure their boredom, but the cure doesn't last long, especially when the man takes a walk, as Harold always did. The other three are just names he waved at me. There were others, too, but these are the only ones I remember."

I wondered if Harold had a condom dispenser with notches carved on it. I said, "Harold must have spent a lot of money going back and forth on the ferry. Was he seen on it the day Ollie was killed?"

"I have no idea. But if he was or wasn't it wouldn't mean anything because the beach was still open then and anyone with an SUV could have come and gone that way."

"That's Harold's blue Cherokee out in the barn?"

"Yes."

"If Harold wasn't with a woman that night, where was he?"

She put down her coffee cup. "It's maddening. He wouldn't tell me. I've wracked my brain trying to guess, but it's hopeless. It wasn't like Harold to be secretive about his sexual exploits or any of his other bad habits. He liked to tell me about them, in fact, because he knew I didn't like hearing about those parts of his life." She took a breath and let it out. "My son didn't love me as much as I loved him. I think it started while he watched his father drink himself to death. I suspect that Harold, who was just a boy then, decided that I had killed him, that I somehow was responsible."

"Maybe one of his women friends will know something," I said. "A lot of confidences are exchanged in bed."

"You have to love and trust someone to

tell them secrets," said Maud. "My son wasn't the loving and trusting type. Self-interest was his specialty, I'm afraid."

"He didn't mind writing letters supporting CHOA's views."

Her hard, old face got harder. "I think that was to make himself seem more important, not because he really believed any of the things he said."

"You don't have a very high opinion of your son," I said.

"I love him and I'll miss him, but I have no illusions about him. He was a selfish, sometimes cruel man."

"So you don't think he was protecting someone else when he wouldn't say where he'd been?"

"I think he was protecting himself."

I asked the logical question. "From what? Murder, perhaps?"

"No! He was cruel, but it was a petty cruelty. He didn't have the backbone to commit murder or even to strike someone. He attacked me with words but never raised a hand to me. He was a physical coward. He was tall and handsome, but he had no real courage and he let himself get fat and mean."

"What was he hiding, then?"

"I don't know. Something too taboo

even for him to want known, maybe. But he was so shameless that I can't imagine what that could be."

"Maybe he wanted to protect someone or something he loved. Even Hitler loved dogs and opera."

She shook her head. "I never heard him speak about love. Not in his whole life. He didn't even love sex. He lusted after it. Lust isn't love."

I wondered if lust was as close as Harold got to love or whether, in spite of the evidence to the contrary, he had feelings that not even his mother knew about. Totally loveless people do exist, but they're very rare.

I didn't think I was going to get much more from Maud Mayhew, so I rose and thanked her for her time.

"I'll keep you informed if I learn anything," I said at the door.

"Harold didn't kill Ollie Mattes. I know he didn't."

I hedged. "I have no reason to think that he did."

"What are you going to do now?"

"I'm going to talk to the women on that list you gave me. Can you tell me where the two on Chappy live?"

She could and did, but then sniffed and

added, "They'll lie if it suits their purpose."

"Most of us do," I said, feeling tired by her fatigue and irked by her cynicism.

The two women who lived on Chappaquiddick were Glenda Harper and Anthea Burns. I'd never heard of either one of them, but followed Maud Mayhew's directions and found a mailbox marked HARPER on Litchfield Road.

The driveway beside the mailbox led west and ended on a low bluff overlooking Katama Bay just south of the narrows. The house was a middle-aged one, younger than the Mayhew house but older than many others. The view to the west, over the water, was excellent, and a path led down to a private beach with a dock at one end. Tied to the dock were a daysailer about seventeen feet long and a mini-cigarette boat with an outsized outboard.

I loathe overpowered motorboats but the daysailer looked good. As I admired it a young woman came out of the house and gave me a questioning look.

"May I help you?"

She was in her midtwenties and had a smooth tan. She wore casual rich girl clothes and her eyes assessed me down to the last ounce.

"My name is Jackson," I said. "I'm looking for Glenda Harper."

She smiled. "I'm Glenda Harper."

I smiled back and made a sweeping gesture with my hand. "Nice place you have here, Miss Harper."

"It's Mrs. Harper. Yes, we like it. What can I do for you, Mr. Jackson?"

I turned back to her and noticed for the first time the small rounding of her belly. "I may want to speak to your husband, too, Mrs. Harper. Is he in?"

Her smile became artificial. "I hope you're not another of those people looking to buy real estate, Mr. Jackson, because if you are, you can leave right now. Our place isn't for sale, and my husband would tell you the same thing if he was here."

"It's just as well that he isn't," I said, maintaining my own fraudulent smile. "I don't want to talk about real estate; I want to talk about Harold Hobbes."

Her smile disappeared a fraction of a second before mine did, and she seemed to pale a shade or two beneath her tan. Her hand touched her throat.

"I don't know what you mean."

"I just came from talking with Maud Mayhew," I said. "I think you know what I mean."

15

There was a bench overlooking the beach and the bay. I gestured toward it. "Let's sit down over here where we can be comfortable." I walked to it and sat down. The bright sun was on my left shoulder. Out in the bay small boats were frolicking in the gentle wind. On the far side of the bay, across from the Katama boat landing, I could see people digging for clams and raking for quahogs. It was a classic Vineyard morning, just the sort that greatly pleases the chamber of commerce.

For a minute I thought that Glenda Harper was going to ignore my invitation to join me, but then I heard her approach. She sat on the far end of the bench.

"What do you want?" Her voice darted at me like the tongue of a snake. "If you're after money, you won't get it!"

"I don't want money, I want information. Does your husband know about you

187

and Harold Hobbes?"

"There's nothing to know about Harold Hobbes and me."

I looked at her and saw fury and fear in her face. "You don't have to lie to me," I said. "I don't care about your private life. It's none of my business. I'm investigating the death of Harold Hobbes. You were lovers. I want to talk to you about some times you might have been together."

"We were never lovers! We were never together!"

"Harold told his mother otherwise."

"He lied!"

"Is that his child you're carrying?"

"How dare you! Go away!"

But though her voice ordered me gone, she didn't stand or gesture. Instead, she sat and stared wide-eyed at the bay. I could almost see energy slipping away from her.

I changed gears. "I need your help," I said. "I'm trying to find out where Harold Hobbes was the evening Ollie Mattes was killed. I thought he might have been with you."

"Are you going to tell my husband about this?" Her voice had become almost unnaturally calm. It reminded me somehow of that odd, breathless air and the peculiar yellow sky that you sometimes experience

188

before the arrival of a hurricane.

"I don't plan to," I said. "Was Harold with you that evening?"

She seemed to have fallen into a dream. Her anger was gone and her face was peaceful. "No. We were through with each other months ago. The flame didn't burn long. It started because Jim, that's my husband, spent a lot of time away on business and I was angry with him for going and Harold was here and interested." She shrugged. "I think it was a kind of revenge for me."

I nodded. "Since he kept leaving you for money, you got even by taking a lover?"

"Yes. And at first being with Harold made me feel excited and more alive, but that didn't last long. Jim came home and told me that he'd decided to cut down on his traveling and stay closer to home. He was so innocent and decent that all my deceptions and lies got to be too much. Harold and I tired of each other about the same time and then it was just over. And I was glad." She looked at me with distant eyes. "Before long it was as though it had never happened. I should have known that Harold would tell someone."

"He told his mother, at least, and she told me."

"Yes. And now you'll tell someone. I wonder what Jim will do when he learns."

I couldn't imagine him not knowing, since so many other people probably did, but all I said was, "He won't learn anything from me. Who did Harold go to after he left you? Do you know?"

She nodded and gave me a crooked smile. "Oh, yes. Anthea Burns was next. She told me so herself. He was a conquest, and some women like to talk about such things. Of course that was before he left her, too. He was a traveling man, as they say. The last I heard he was with some woman up in Chilmark."

"He told his mother about Anthea, too. And about at least three other women."

"What a nice son. He told his mother everything."

Her irony lacked the bitterness I would have expected. Her tone was almost one of amusement. I liked her for her total lack of self-pity.

I asked, "Where were you and your husband the night Ollie Mattes was killed?"

She looked pleasantly puzzled. "Why, right here. I remember it very well. It was a nice night and there was a gentle wind. We sat here on this bench and I told him about the baby. He was surprised and we were both happy. Why do you ask?"

"I hoped that you might have been somewhere else; out on North Neck, for instance."

She appeared honestly surprised rather than offended. "You think one of us might have killed Ollie Mattes? Why would either of us do a thing like that? We didn't even know him!"

"I hoped you might have seen something or someone out there."

"Well, we didn't. We were here."

"Can you prove it?" I asked.

Her amusement went away. "No, Mr. Jackson, there were no witnesses. I don't like that question!"

"You won't like this one either, but I have to ask you, because both you and your husband have reason to dislike Harold Hobbes. Where were you two the night Harold was killed?"

She was still angry, but confident this time. "We have about thirty witnesses to where we were that night, and one of them is Maud Mayhew! We were at a CHOA meeting. Anthea Burns was there as well, in case you plan to browbeat her, too."

I had been giving that possibility thought, in fact.

"What was the meeting about?"

191

"It was about stopping the building of the Pierson house, if you must know."

"Did anybody have any ideas that hadn't already been tried?"

"No! And don't start thinking that somebody at CHOA killed Ollie Mattes, because that didn't happen!"

"Harold Hobbes trashed the windows in Pierson's house, and he was a CHOA member."

"If he did, he did it on his own. CHOA would never do such a thing!"

"Do you have any idea why Harold wasn't at the meeting?"

"No." She lifted her chin. "But knowing Harold, I'd guess he was with a woman somewhere."

"If he was, why didn't he tell his mother? He told her about his other women, including you."

She brushed at her hair and frowned and looked out over the bay. "I don't know."

I got up. "If the police haven't already been here, it's possible that they'll come to ask you questions like the ones I've asked. Don't be afraid, because if what you've told me is true, it seems to me that you and your husband are in the clear."

"It's true. Everything I told you is true."

I left her there and drove away, hoping

that I wasn't as cruel a person as I suspected I could be.

I drove to Pocha Road, and not far after the pavement ended and the road became dirt I found Anthea Burns's mailbox. There was a huge new house being built nearby and its owner had cut down a swath of trees to improve his view of the sea. It was exactly the sort of home that CHOA people didn't want built on their sometimes island and was so close to the road that it couldn't be overlooked. Being one who is often astounded but rarely if ever offended by large houses, I saw it more as a curiosity than a blight on the landscape. But then I wasn't a CHOA person.

Anthea Burns lived in a separate apartment in her parents' house. Her mother, wearing gardening gloves, came into view when I knocked on her door and told me that Anthea was at work in Vineyard Haven.

She squinted up at me. "I'll tell her you came by, Mr. . . . ?"

"Jackson. My friends call me J.W."

"Are you the Jackson who doesn't think plovers should be allowed to fledge on Norton's Point Beach?"

Uh, oh. Trouble at River City. "I'm a Jackson who doesn't think off-road vehi-

cles are any danger to the plover popula-
tion and that the beach should stay open
all summer."

She surprised me by smiling. "I agree
with you, Mr. Jackson."

"I thought you CHOA people all
thought the other way."

"I'm not a member of CHOA. Anthea is,
but I'm not. I think the CHOAs are a
bunch of rich NIMBYs who aren't worth
the time of day. Of course Anthea dis-
agrees with me. Do you have a message
you'd like to leave for her, Mr. Jackson?"

"No, but I'd like to talk to her for a few
minutes. Can you tell me where she works?"

She could and she did. "You mind
telling me why you want to see her, Mr.
Jackson?"

"I don't mind, but she might. When you
were her age, did you want your mother to
know everything you talked about, or everyone you knew, or everything you did?"

She laughed and stood back. "No, I
guess not. You've gotten me curious,
though."

"That killed the cat, but I don't think
you're in any danger. I'll leave it up to her
to tell you if she wants to. Maybe you
should ask her when she gets home."

"Ha!"

I drove back to the ferry. The line of cars on the far side was long. The line on the Chappy side was short. When I got on board I asked the captain if she remembered Harold Hobbes's car. She said sure, he drove a blue Cherokee. Too bad about Harold.

It was a bit after noon, so I went home and had a Sam Adams and a bluefish salad sandwich. Then, since nature never stops for murder, I went out and weeded our gardens for a couple of hours. While I weeded I thought things over. Just before three I washed up and drove to Vineyard Haven.

16

Anthea Burns worked in the office of a building supplies place on Beach Road. The office doors were open as such doors always seem to be at places that sell the stuff it takes to build a house. I thought it ironic that she, who actively opposed development on Chappaquiddick, worked in such a business. But maybe she only sold lumber to up-islanders.

I asked the guy at the counter if I could speak to her and before turning to his next customer he waved me into the office and called, "Anthea, there's a guy here who wants to see you!"

Anthea Burns turned out to be a pretty young woman sitting behind a computer and surrounded by invoices and other pieces of paper. She wore no rings on her left hand but she did wear large glasses that would never prevent passes. Behind them, her eyes were long-lashed and blue.

She smiled up at me.

"May I help you?"

She was alone in the office and the guy outside was busy with his customer, so I stepped close to her desk and spoke quietly and quickly.

"My name is Jackson. I'm investigating the death of Harold Hobbes. Your name came up as someone who knew him fairly well. I know you were at a CHOA meeting the night he was killed, so you're not a suspect in his murder, but if you know of any enemies he might have had I'd like to know their names."

She flicked a glance at the door, then back at me. Her voice was barely more than a whisper. "I don't know what you mean. I'm working. I don't have time to talk to you now!"

I leaned toward her and lowered my own voice still more but made it hard. "I'm working, too. You and Harold Hobbes were lovers and lovers often confide in each other. All I want from you are the names of any enemies he might have mentioned, any people who might have wished him harm. Give me those names and I'll be happy and gone. Give me grief and I'll talk louder."

She threw another look at the office

door, beyond which the counterman was still involved with his customer. She closed those long-lashed eyes and took a moment to decide, then looked at me as her voice came in a rush, like water from an opened sluice. I had the impression that she had been saving her words for a long time and was glad to let them pour out.

"He never mentioned any enemies but he had them. You can start with the women he left in his wake. I'm one of them. And you might try the husbands and boyfriends. None of them had a reason to wish Harold well! Harold used everyone he met. If he had any friends at all, I don't know who they were! I didn't kill him, but I didn't cry when I got the news that someone else had."

"Give me some names."

"Sure. Try Glenda and Jim Harper for two. Glenda was my predecessor."

"They were both at the CHOA meeting that night."

"Maybe they hired a hit man."

"Maybe you did."

Her mouth twisted into a sort of smile. "Where do you find a hit man, anyway? I'm afraid I don't know any."

"I doubt if the Harpers do, either."

"All right, why don't you talk to Maria

198

Danawa or Kristen Kolle or Anita Pereira?"

They were the other three names Maud Mayhew had given me. "Doesn't Anita Pereira run Black Pony Farm?"

"That's Anita, all right."

"Who's Kristen Kolle, and where can I find her?"

"Harold left me for Maria Danawa, then went from her to Kristen, and then left Kristen for Anita. Harold was quite a lady-killer. Maria's single and Kristen's divorced, but Anita has a husband who may have decided he didn't like sharing his wife with Harold." She told me where Kristen Kolle lived. "You'll find both ladies up there in Chilmark," she said. "Chilmark was Harold's new hunting grounds after he'd gone through all the game over on Chappy and down-island."

I straightened. "You have a good jungle telegraph."

She shrugged. "Word gets around."

"Can you think of any other names?"

The counterman chose that moment to come in through the door. "Anthea, can you give me a copy of the invoice for the Joslyn job?"

"Sure," she said. I stepped away from her desk and she dug through a stack of papers. "Here you go." She gave him the invoice and he thanked her and went back to the counter.

"You want other names," she said to me, "you talk with Harold's mother. They say he told her everything."

"He wouldn't tell her where he was the night Ollie Mattes was killed, and he wasn't at the CHOA meeting that last night. Any idea where he might have been?"

"In some woman's bed?"

"Up in Chilmark?"

She spread her hands. "The home of his last known conquests, but maybe he'd moved on to greener pastures."

"If he was with another woman, why didn't he tell Maud about her? He told her about all the others."

She nodded. "Including me. Maybe he was with a pig in a sty and was ashamed to admit it. Everybody is ashamed of something. What are you ashamed of, Mr. Jackson?"

"I'll never tell," I said. I thanked her for her time and left. I found myself hoping that she'd find herself a better man than Harold Hobbes. My watch told me that I had enough time for interviews with a couple more people before I headed home to cook supper. The closest one was Maria Danawa, the daughter of a friend and the only one of Harold Hobbes's women I actually knew fairly well.

Maria worked as a nurse in Oak Bluffs, down the hall from where Zee plied the same trade in the ER. As far as I knew, Marie was currently being wooed by Paul Fox, who was one of the island's many realtors. There are about fifteen thousand full-time residents on Martha's Vineyard, and nine out of ten of them are realtors who are busy selling properties to off-islanders, since not many of the remaining 10 percent of full-time residents can afford to buy land. Paul was not the first man in Maria's life, however. She was a slim young blonde who had no trouble being attractive to men, including me. I'm very married but not blind.

I drove to the hospital and found her.

"Hi, J.W.," she said, smiling. "What brings you here? Are you sick?"

"Just nosy. Can I talk with you for a minute? In private?"

"You've roused my curiosity." She glanced around. "Come on." I followed her into an empty office. "How can I help you?"

"I'm trying to get a line on Harold

Hobbes's past life. I know you two dated, and I'm wondering if he ever mentioned anyone who might have had a grudge against him."

Her pretty face hardened. "I can tell you that I sure as hell did! He not only dumped me, he laughed when he did it!" Then she took a deep breath. "But if you think I killed him, you're wrong. I got over Harold pretty fast and called myself lucky."

It was a healthy response. "I know you didn't kill him," I said. "I'm just trying to get a name to chase. Someone who might actually have hated him enough to have done it. Did he ever say anything about anybody like that?"

Her smile was hard. "How about his other women? How about their brothers and fathers and boyfriends? I don't know many of their names, but you can probably get a list. You might start with Kristen Kolle. I understand that he shed her as fast as he shed me. Maybe she carried a grudge farther than I did."

"I'll ask her," I said. "How are things with Paul?"

She brightened. "Fine. Nothing like they were with Harold. Even my mother likes him. Look at this."

I looked. A bigger diamond than any I

could afford gleamed on the ring finger of her left hand. The real estate business was a good one, apparently.

Being one who approves of marriage, I offered her my sincere best wishes, accepted her thanks, and left.

Kristen Kolle lived off North Road not far from Tabor House Road. There'd been Tabors on the island in the 1600s, but I didn't know which member of the family had owned the house that had given the road its name. Would there ever be a Jackson House Road? Probably not.

There was no Kolle Road either, but there was a Kolle driveway. I wondered if a merry old soul lived at the end of it. When I got to the house the only person there was a teenaged boy pushing a lawn mower around the yard. He didn't look too merry and was glad to stop when I approached him and asked if Kristen was home.

"No," he said. "Mom drove Grandma to the codger game."

"I hate to admit to my ignorance," I said, "but what's the codger game?"

"Oh," said the boy. "It's the old ladies' slow-pitch-softball game. You have to be sixty to play. Grandma plays second base for the Chilmark Crushers. They play once a week and today's the day."

He told me where to find the field and I drove there and parked beside a familiar-looking SUV in a line of cars along the third-base line.

A baseball diamond with well-worn baselines and a high backstop for balls that got past the catcher occupied a flat green field. Elderly women wearing red baseball caps and baseball gloves were scattered around the infield and outfield. There were apparently six outfielders and six infielders along with a pitcher and catcher.

At bat was a lanky woman with white hair sticking out from under a blue cap. Other gray-haired women wearing red caps sat on a bench outside of the first-base line. Women with blue caps sat outside the third-base line.

There were no bleachers, but women and men stood behind the benches and beside cars. I stood behind the team with blue caps.

"Hit it, Blanche!"

"No-hitter! No-hitter!"

Blanche topped a fat pitch down the third-base line and beat out a throw by an infielder who had played too deep.

"Atta girl, Blanche! Come on, Sarah, knock her in!"

"Long ball! Long ball! Play back!"

The right fielders limped deeper and Sarah, carrying what looked like a brand-new bat, strolled to the plate. Clearly she was a feared slugger. It wasn't until she took her southpaw stance that I recognized her as Sarah Bradford. The last time I'd seen her she'd been dressed in riding togs. Now she sported a baseball cap and sneakers. Sarah the jock.

She took two pitches and hit the third one over the outermost outfielder, and two runs were home just like that. As the two runners were greeted by their teammates I saw that there was a red C on the front of each blue cap. I was standing behind the bench of the Chilmark Crushers, one of whom was the mother of Kristen Kolle. I looked around for Kristen.

I didn't know what she looked like, but there were several women in the crowd who seemed to be about the right age to be the daughter of a player and the mother of the kid with the lawn mower. I went to one of them and asked if she was Kristen. She wasn't but she pointed to the woman who was and I went over to her.

She was shouting at a woman carrying a bat to the plate. "Come on, Mom! Smack that ball!"

I watched while Mom fouled one pitch

off, missed the next, and then smacked the third right into the pitcher's mitt. The pitcher looked surprised but pleased to find the ball in her possession.

"Oh, drat! Nice try. Next time!"

Mom tapped the ground with her bat and walked cheerfully back to the bench.

"Mrs. Kolle?"

I could see her boy's face in hers. They both had high cheekbones, firm jaws, and light brown eyes.

"Yes?"

"It's a game of inches," I said. "A foot either way and the ball's past the pitcher and your mother's on first."

"It's possible. She can't slug like Sarah Bradford, but she has a good glove and she can make the throw to first. Have we met?"

"No." I told her my name. "Can I have a few words with you in private?"

She looked wary. "What about?"

I told her. When her face paled and anger entered her eyes, I said, "I won't take much of your time. Maybe we can talk over by your car, where we can be alone."

Her firm jaw got firmer, but she nodded and led the way to a newish Chevy sedan parked not far from my own Land Cruiser.

"Harold and I split months ago," she said. "I wish we'd never met at all."

"You're not the first woman he charmed."

"Nor the last. Looking back I can't imagine why I didn't see him for what he really was."

"What was he?"

"A good-looking guy with some money, a smooth talker, a man who knew what women liked to hear, who knew how to touch them. I saw all that, all right. I just didn't see the meanness underneath. That came later."

"Did he hurt you?"

"Not with his hands; with his mouth. And I don't think it was just me. I think he hated all women. He liked to use them and then make them feel like soiled clothes and drop them. At least that's what happened to me. I was a fool."

"Has anyone asked you where you were the evening he was killed?"

Her brown eyes widened then narrowed. "Is that what this is about? Do you think I killed him? Well, I didn't. I'd gotten his stench off of me by then and I certainly wasn't going to dirty my hands again."

"Can you tell me where you were that evening?"

"I was at home with my mother and my son. But I can tell you something else that might interest you. I can tell you where

Harold Hobbes was that day, in the late afternoon. As I was driving home I saw him and a woman pull out of Old County Road ahead of me and then go off on South Road. I don't think he recognized my car but I recognized that blue Jeep he drove."

"Did you recognize the woman?"

"No. I didn't see her face, but it was a woman, all right. If she was Harold's latest, she was also his last, I'd say."

"What time did you see them?"

"I was coming home from work in Edgartown, so it must have been about five." She looked at me with a steady gaze. "His mother found his body about four hours later, according to the papers. No loss, as far as I'm concerned."

"Don't you want to know who killed him?"

"I don't approve of murder, but this one was overdue. Are we through here?"

"Just two more questions. Do you have any ideas about who might have wanted Harold dead?"

"You mean besides me and every other woman he slept with and a few husbands and boyfriends? No. But I wouldn't be surprised if there were some others. What else can I tell you?"

"Did you know Ollie Mattes?"

She looked puzzled. "No. I read about him in the papers. Why?"

"Just wondering. Do you know Ron Pierson?"

"That's three questions. No, I don't know Ron Pierson. I've read about his big house, but he and I don't frequent the same social circles. Now, if you'll excuse me."

She turned and walked back to the ball game, and I went back to my truck. There I remembered where I'd seen the SUV I'd parked beside. It had been hooked to a horse trailer in Cheryl Bradford's yard. I was next to Sarah Bradford's wheels. I looked around but saw no sign of Cheryl's car or of Cheryl. I got into the Land Cruiser and went home to save my family from death by starvation.

17

That evening, before and after supper, Zee and the kids took turns playing with our new computer. I watched them, full of increasing doubt that I would ever be able to manipulate it without having an instructor peering over my shoulder and guiding my every move.

"Don't worry, Pa," said little Diana as she headed off to bed. "It's hard at first but then you get good at it."

"Thanks, sweetie." I gave her a good-night kiss.

"She's right, you know," said Zee, coming to where I was seated and reading my *Computers for Idiots* book. "You just have to keep at it. It's like driving a car. You don't have to know why it works the way it does, all you have to know is how to run it."

"I was a danger to my father's car all the time he was teaching me to drive, and the first time I soloed I ran into a tree. I don't want to hit the wrong key and wreck this machine."

"Well, even if you manage to run the computer into a tree, it will probably survive. Watch the kids. They're fearless. If they do something that screws things up they just keep pecking away until everything's right again."

"I think I'll read this book about how to do what I want to do instead of just finding out as I go."

"You're the product of a bygone century, Jefferson, and I guess you'll never change."

I put down my book and ran my hands down over her hips. "Nice," I said. "Some things are timeless." Between the top of her shorts and the bottom of the shirt she had tied around her waist was a strip of flat belly. I leaned forward and gave it a lick. She ran her hands through my hair.

"I'll show you more tongue tricks later," I said. "Meanwhile, though, check me out while I try to get myself onto the Internet. I want to see if I can remember what I've just been reading."

"I can do that," said Zee. And she did. "See," she said when I got there, "that wasn't hard. Anything you'd like to check out, now that you're here in cyberspace?"

I thought for a moment. "How about sound systems?"

"Sound systems? Are you interested in buying a sound system?"

"No, but I'd like to know how the Silencer wrecks them. Maybe he learned how to do it on the Internet."

She lifted her eyebrows. "Could be, I guess. Well, let's find out. Move your cursor up here and type in 'sound systems.' "

I did that and up came a page telling me that I was looking at the first ten sites out of more than 3,300,000. Not an encouraging start.

I clicked on one of the sites and then another and learned that I could buy such things as the world's loudest car audio system, a set of device drivers that would provide a uniform API across all of the major UNIK architecture, or other systems that were described by capitalized initials whose meanings the advertisers saw no need to explain.

I tried a half dozen more sites and was offered more marvels of the electronic arts. A lot of people wanted to sell me sound systems but no one seemed to be selling information on how to destroy one.

I carefully and successfully extracted

myself from cyberspace. I was exhausted.

Zee patted me on the back. "Well done, thou good and faithful servant. You went out there and got back again in one piece. It's what we gobs call a successful cruise. Of course you didn't find what you were looking for, but what the heck."

I abandoned the computer and pulled her down on my lap. "This will do as a substitute," I said, running a hand up her thigh.

The next morning I was back in Chilmark.

Anita Pereira lived on Black Pony Farm, not too far from the Bradford place on South Road. She and her husband, Mack, were part of the considerable group of islanders whose lives revolved around horses. They stabled horses and offered trail rides and training for equestrian competitions. I'd seen the Pereiras with their horses and students at the county fair and in the Fourth of July parades. That was about as close as I preferred to get to horses.

The Pereiras, I recalled, were both about forty and both sported shiny black hair and pleasant faces. I found Anita down by their indoor riding arena and saw him in a far corral apparently instructing a girl on a pony the art of steeplechasing.

Anita gave me an evaluative glance and smiled. "May I help you, Mr. . . . ?"

"Jackson. My friends call me J.W." I told her the story I'd told so many others: of my investigation into the death of Harold Hobbes. "You were mentioned as someone who was close to him," I said. "I'm trying to find out who might have disliked him enough to kill him."

"We were lovers, Mr. Jackson, but he didn't whisper his enemies' names in my ear while we were having sex. Is that what you had in mind?" Her smile widened. "I hope I haven't shocked you. My husband and I have a very open marriage. He doesn't mind my men and I don't mind his women."

"I'm not shocked," I said, barely managing not to be.

"You looked shocked but now you're smiling. I'm glad." She gestured toward my wedding band. "I see that you're a married man, but do you swing?"

"Is that still the term that's used? No, my swinging days are long past. Now one woman is all I can handle."

"Then I can only hope that you're all the man that your wife can handle. Are you?" Her smile was wider and bolder and full of good humor.

"She's the one who would know that. We're in the book and she'll be home about suppertime if you want to phone and ask her. Her name is Zeolinda. Zee, for short."

"Oh, Zee Jackson. Is she your wife? I know her. She works at the emergency room in the hospital. I've taken a few of our students there when they proved to be worse riders than they claimed. She's very beautiful. Far prettier than I am, certainly." She tipped her head to one side, still smiling. "She has the look of a woman who has a good man."

"I'm glad to hear that. Do you know of anyone who might have wanted Harold Hobbes dead?"

"If I were you, I might think that Mack and I were logical suspects, but I'm me and I know we don't qualify."

"Maybe Mack isn't as indifferent to your lovers as you think."

"But Harold and I stopped being lovers a month ago. He found a new woman and I found a new man and Mack hasn't shown the slightest interest in killing anyone. Mack isn't the killing type. He just likes to have sex with women, including me."

"Maybe you were mad at Harold for leaving you."

"You're funnier than you think. Harold was a hard worker in bed but he was a little too mechanical for my tastes. You know what I mean? He was a real stud, but that's about all, and after the rides were over we were both glad to kiss and say good-bye. Are you sure you don't swing?"

"I'm sure. Do you know the name of the woman he took up with after he left you?"

"Do you think you might change your mind? We could have a good time together."

"I don't doubt it for a minute, but I don't expect to change my mind. You'd probably give me a heart attack. What's the woman's name?"

"Funny you should mention a heart attack, because that's just what they say happened to Cheryl's father. Died of a heart attack having sex with a woman he wasn't married to. Not a bad way to go, I'd say. Cheryl Bradford. She lives right down the road. You know her? Say, I think I've given you two shocks in five minutes."

"More reason for me not to climb into the sack with you. You're a danger to me before you even get your clothes off. I've met Cheryl Bradford. Are you sure they were lovers? How do you know?"

She spread her hands. "What's not to

know? Cheryl is my best friend. We tell each other everything. When he left me, he went to her and everyone was happy. Say, if you're not interested in sex with me, how about renting one of our horses and taking a couple of riding lessons? If you buy yourself a Stetson and some high-heeled boots you could pass for a cowboy."

"Your first offer was a lot more tempting. Horses and I don't get along. Do you think Cheryl might have hated Harold enough to kill him?"

"Cheryl? Not a chance."

"He was a rolling stone. Maybe he left her for another woman just like he left all of his other conquests. Not everybody is as casual about these breakups as you are."

She was cheerful. "As far as I know they were still sharing sheets when he got himself killed. Cheryl doesn't have too much going on between her ears but she's not the murdering type. Now, if her mother had known about Harold, she might have done him in. Sarah hates men in general, and even though Harold wasn't as much of a man as he thought he was, he was still a man. Sarah might have plugged him on general principles."

"Harold wasn't shot; he was beaten to death with a blunt instrument."

"Whatever. In any case, Sarah still doesn't know about Cheryl and Harold. Cheryl made me swear not to tell her, and of course I didn't. I hope you won't either. Cheryl's already got grief enough. She doesn't need Sarah browbeating her and bad-mouthing the man she loved."

"Why is Sarah Bradford so down on men?"

"I guess she got soured by her husband's lifestyle. Not everybody's like me and Mack."

Very true. "Did you know Ollie Mattes?"

"According to the grapevine, Ollie was the result of old man Bradford's last act on earth. I don't think I ever saw him, though."

"How about Ron Pierson?"

"Sarah was a Pierson and I think that Ron is her nephew, or something like that. I hear Sarah doesn't like him any better than she likes any other men. In fact, maybe she hates him more, because they say there's a Pierson family feud of some kind, and fights in families can be the worst kind."

"Ron Pierson is building the house where Ollie Mattes was killed. Ollie got his head mashed in just like Harold Hobbes did. You have any thoughts about any of that?"

"You bet. It makes me glad I live here with Mack in Chilmark and not down there on Chappaquiddick where people kill each other with sticks."

I drove away feeling improved by my contact with Anita Pereira. Her combination of good nature and shameless sensualism was a tonic, and her thoughts about Harold and about women had given rise to thoughts of my own.

18

I drove down the Bradfords' driveway for a second time in a week after never having been there before during my many years on the Vineyard. I was conscious, and not for the first time, that there was a lot more of this little island that I'd never seen than I *had* seen or probably ever would see, because like many places that looked small on a map, it was bigger than it seemed. I remembered once reading that if you gave every person in the world two square feet of earth to stand on, you could put all of them on Martha's Vineyard.

Beyond the farm buildings and the green fields where horses grazed, the blue Atlantic reached away toward a misty southern horizon and lines of rolling, white-topped breakers crumbled against the sand.

The first Bradford on this land had probably been one of those combination farmer-fishermen like so many other people who live near the oceans of the world and make a hard living from the unforgiving land and sea. The current generation seemed to have progressed well beyond that tough start and become the inheritors of wealth sufficient to make them gentlemen and gentlewomen who didn't have to work for a living.

One indication of this was the figure of a woman in riding clothes coming along a bridle path toward the barn. I recognized her at once as Cheryl Bradford. Not too many working people take cross-country rides in the middle of the morning.

I drove into the yard and saw that her mother's SUV was missing. Maybe Mom had a job. Too bad, because I wanted to talk with both Bradfords. But I could start with Cheryl, so I walked down to the barn, where I found her putting away her saddle and blanket and preparing to currycomb her horse. I stayed outside the stall holding her and the horse.

"Mr. Jackson. What brings you here again?"

"I neglected to ask you some questions I hope you'll answer now."

She began to curry her horse. "That depends upon the questions, I guess. Let's hear them."

"I wasn't quite frank with you when we spoke before. I'm investigating Harold Hobbes's death."

Her currycomb paused and then moved on. "What's that got to do with me?"

"You and he were lovers, and you were with him just before his body was found."

"That's a lie!"

People lie about the truth and they lie about lies. I've done it myself more than once. "No, it isn't," I said. "If the police don't already know about your relationship with him, you'll be a prime suspect in his murder when they find out."

She sagged against the horse. "You can't be serious."

"I am. Harold was the love-'em-and-leave-'em kind of man. There were a lot of women in his life and you were the last one. You wouldn't be the first jilted woman to kill her man."

She gave up the pose of innocence. She lowered the currycomb and put her arms around her horse's neck, laying her head against its warm skin. I was aware of the sweet barn smell of straw and leather.

"No. He wasn't leaving me. We loved one another. We made plans that last night. We were going to go away together. Get away from the people we know here and start a new life somewhere else where we could be happy."

It was a different story than I'd gotten from Hobbes's other women. He had never promised a new life with any of them.

"You're in trouble," I said, "so don't lie to me. Harold Hobbes used women and dropped them. He did it again and again. He never loved anybody."

Her voice was weak but angry. "You're cruel and you're wrong. He was kind and gentle and he loved me. He did!" She began to cry. "And now he's dead and my life is empty. I feel like I'm living in my own tomb."

I studied her. Her face was buried in the slick hair of her horse's neck and her shoulders were shaking. The horse turned its head slightly and looked down at her before turning away again. Its eyes were gentle and curious.

"Why did you want to lie to me about your relationship?"

Her voice sounded wet. "Because you could tell my mother and I don't want her to know. She didn't like my husband and she's never liked any of the men I've dated. I don't want her saying things about Harold that she said about them! Please don't tell her! Please!"

"I won't. But I'm not the only one who knows. I've talked with Anita Pereira."

"Anita! Anita wouldn't tell Mother."

"You're probably right, but she told me."

"I don't think I could stand Mother knowing. My father was a philanderer. You probably know that. My mother hasn't trusted any man since."

"Not even your brother?"

"He's her son but he's a man. She's not warm toward him because he's got our father's blood in him, but he's her son so she tries to treat him fairly, at least. I think he'd love to be closer to her but she won't allow it."

The Bradford family had more than its share of problems.

"Somebody killed Harold at his own house," I said. "Do you have any idea who might have done it? Did he mention any enemies?"

"No. He didn't try to hide his past, but he said he'd changed. Something had happened to him that had never happened before. The something was me, he said. I know about his other women, and Anita and I have talked, but Harold wasn't the man Anita described. I think he wanted us to leave here so he could get completely away from his past and we could start

224

again together. I know people must have disliked him, but he never mentioned any names."

"Did he tell you that he was the one who broke all of the windows in Ron Pierson's house?"

She wiped at her eyes and nodded. "It was another reason for us to leave. Especially after Ollie Mattes was killed. Harold was sure that if anyone found out about the windows they'd think he'd gone back again and killed Ollie. But he didn't!"

I could almost hear the click in my mind. "You know he didn't because he was with you that evening."

"Yes, yes. We were together all afternoon and into the evening."

"He wouldn't tell his mother where he'd been. Do you know why?"

"No. I would have testified that we were together, even if it meant my mother would learn about us. But he wouldn't have it. He told me never to tell anyone. He said we'd go away and no one would ever find us."

I thought about the number of windows that had been broken in the Pierson house. "Someone was with him the night he broke those windows," I said. "Do you know who it was?"

She never hesitated. "Yes. It was me. Harold was very emotional about people wrecking Chappy, and he was set on showing Ron Pierson he wasn't wanted by smashing those windows, and I was worried about him so I went too. Then when he started crashing all that glass and making all that noise, I was afraid someone would hear and come and find him, so I found another hammer in his car and went and broke as many windows as I could as fast as I could. I know I was wrong but I did it because I wanted us to get away."

"So you weren't his only passion."

She let go of her horse's neck and looked at me. "No. But I was his best." Her eyes were red but there was something like pride in her voice. "Do you think I should have told the police what I did? I didn't tell them that when they talked with me. I caused a lot of damage."

I thought about Ron Pierson's money. He could afford to replace his windows. "If you do that," I said, "you'll have to tell the police that Harold was involved too. And then you'll have to tell them about your relationship. And then your mother will learn about it if she doesn't already know. I think I'd keep my mouth shut, if I were you."

"You're not going to tell them?"

I've done worse things than vandalize windows. "Not unless I have a better reason than I have now," I said. "You were seen later at the Pierson place. The police must have asked you about that. Why did you go back?"

"They did ask me. I told them it was because my half brother, Ollie, had been killed there and I wanted to see where it happened. The real reason was in case Harold or I had left some clue that could be traced back to us. Who saw me?"

"No one who knew who you were."

"Good." She began to move the currycomb over the horse's shoulder. "Thanks for agreeing to keep my mother in the dark."

"Are you sure she doesn't already know?"

She nodded. "I'm sure. I'd have heard about it by now. She'd have harangued me and made him miserable like she's done with every man who wanted to date me. But she's said nothing. She definitely doesn't know."

"Did Harold have any dangerous habits that you know of? Did he do drugs, for instance? Or was he a gambler?"

"Neither. Why?"

"People in those trades sometimes get violent."

"He drank too much and some people didn't like his politics and he probably left angry women behind him, but he wasn't violent and he didn't have violent associates."

I thought of what Kristen Kolle had told me and took a short intuitive leap. "What did your brother think of you and Harold being together? You two met at his house, didn't you?"

She looked at me in surprise. "How did you know that? Nobody knew that."

It had been a shot in semidarkness but had hit home as such shots sometimes do. "Someone saw you together on Old County Road, coming from the direction of your brother's place," I said. "Why did you meet there and what did your brother think of your relationship?"

She hesitated but she had told me too much to stop now. "We couldn't meet at my house or at Harold's. But Ethan's place is private and we could be alone together. Ethan didn't like it but I'm his sister and I begged him and he let us come there for a few hours at a time. He'd go away and leave us alone and we'd try to be gone before he came home." She touched her knuckles to her mouth. "I'm glad it wasn't Ethan who told you. Except for Anita,

Ethan was the only one who knew about us." She frowned up at me. "He promised he'd never tell anyone, but even before Harold was killed I thought he was getting antsy."

"Secrets are hard to keep," I said.

"But who would he tell? And why? He'd never hurt me and he knew how much Harold meant to me."

"I wouldn't know," I said. "All I know is that he didn't tell me."

Her mood changed. "Harold and I were happy at Ethan's house. We could make love and have a glass of wine on the porch and talk and listen to Vivaldi tapes. Ethan said that Vivaldi wrote four hundred concertos, and he must have had all of them there on his shelves. We listened to them whenever we were there. Do you like Vivaldi, Mr. Jackson?"

"Yes," I said. "But a wag once claimed that Vivaldi really wrote one concerto four hundred times."

She tried but failed to smile at the time-worn jest. "I don't know much about music," she said, "but I know I'll never hear Vivaldi again without thinking about Harold."

Like Margaret in the Goldengrove, it was Cheryl that she mourned for.

19

Passions ran high among the Bradfords, but since Sarah apparently knew nothing of her daughter's love affair with Harold, her general hatred of men seemed an unlikely motive for his murder. Ethan, on the other hand, still seemed a possible suspect, since he did know and disapproved of Harold's liaison with his window-smashing sister.

It was far from impossible that out of love for Cheryl he had coshed Harold to save her from one of the island's most notorious womanizers. People have killed for less reason.

I drove down to the Edgartown Police Station on Pease's Point Way and was told by Kit Goulart, who was tending the desk, that the Chief was in but that he was buried in both routine paperwork and the additional paperwork having to do with the still unsolved murders on Chappaquiddick.

"No problem," I said. "He loves me like a son and will be hurt if I don't drop in to say hello."

"And I'll be fired if you barge in on him, and I'll whack you with my nightstick if you get me fired, so stand right there while I tell him you're here."

Kit and her husband, Joe, both stood over six feet tall and weighed in at 250 or more. You wouldn't want Kit whacking you with her nightstick, if indeed she actually had one. I hadn't seen a nightstick for years, but I wisely took no chances.

"Tell him I've been nosing around in police business," I said as she picked up a phone. "That should get a rise out of him."

"I can imagine," said Kit. She spoke into the phone then put it down and waved toward the Chief's closed office door. "Your father awaits you."

The Chief's desk was piled with paper. As I shut his door behind me he voiced an oft-heard complaint. "Ever since we got computers I've had more paper to deal with. I thought computers were supposed to make paper obsolete."

"You'll be interested to learn that I am now a computer owner myself," I said. "So far I've barely learned how to turn it on and off, but Zee and the kids can make it dance and play games."

"Kids can make them do that without even reading a book," he said. "My grandchildren can probably learn how to build atomic bombs if they want to. Say, maybe I should hire them to come down here and computerize this mess on my desk."

"Nepotism is not unknown in Edgartown," I said, "so why not? They can make a couple bucks and you can go fishing."

He put his hands behind his neck and yawned. "Kit tells me that you've been snooping. No surprise there. What have you learned that I don't already know?"

"Probably nothing, but I'll tell all if you'll do the same."

"Well, I won't, but if you know something I should know you'd better cough it up so I won't be obliged to throw you in jail for some reason or other."

"Being in jail is a pretty good deal these days," I said. "Duane Miller turns out the best meals on the island and I can crawl out a window after supper, spend the night with Zee, and be back in time for breakfast."

"The window has bars on it now, I'm told. Did you hear about the counterfeit bills they found on Mickey Gomes when they collected him in Oak Bluffs?"

"I didn't think Mickey was bright enough to be a counterfeiter."

"And you'd be right. Turns out he got them from a fellow inmate. The story is that while he was outside the walls, Mickey bought some of those prepaid telephone cards for his cellmates and one of them paid him off with queer bills."

"Tsk. So it's true about there being no honor among thieves."

"And guess where the guy got the bills: he made them himself on the jail's computer. No wonder us poor cops are the laughingstock of half the island. If I wasn't wearing the uniform I'd be laughing myself."

"I take it that this means that when you toss me in jail I won't have a computer to play with in my idle hours."

"You got it. No escape window and no computer. Hard times have come to the County of Dukes County Jail."

"Has any inmate sued yet?"

"No, but it's bound to come. Inhumane treatment, police brutality, and all that. They'll probably win their case, too, what with the times being what they are. Now, what do you want? You never come smiling around unless you want something."

"Like I said, I had an info trade in mind.

Just to show I'm playing an honest game I'll start by telling you what I know. Then you can do the same."

"I'm promising nothing but I want everything."

"And that's what you'll get," I lied, and told him almost everything I'd heard or seen in my investigation. Among other things, I didn't burden him with the knowledge that Cheryl Bradford was a window breaker.

"So she and Hobbes were lovers, eh? She didn't tell us that when we interviewed her."

"Was her mother there with her?"

"Yes. So what?"

I told him what Cheryl had told me about hiding the relationship from Sarah. I said, "If you talk with Cheryl privately she'll probably tell you the truth."

He had been a cop a long time and had seen and heard a lot. Like most cops he had considerable sympathy for most people in trouble and an understanding of their fears and weaknesses.

"I'll ask her to come and see me. We can have a private talk. You don't think she killed him?"

I shrugged. "No, but I've been fooled before."

"What about Hobbes's other women? What about their husbands and boy-friends?"

"The only men I've talked to are John Lupien and Ethan Bradford. I haven't scratched them off my list, but I can't link Lupien to Harold Hobbes and I can't link Ethan to Ollie."

"The ME says Mattes and Hobbes were killed with similar weapons by similar assailants. A club or maybe a piece of pipe swung left to right by somebody about middle height. How tall are Lupien and Bradford, would you guess?"

"Both about six feet, I'd say."

"Too tall, according to the ME. We're looking for somebody built lower to the ground. Another thing: Ollie had a fractured skull but he may have still been alive before he got pitched off the cliff. He was only hit once."

"How about Harold?"

"Oh, Harold was very dead before the killer was through with him. Mashed his skull pretty good. Blood all over the place. Harold was a pretty big man, but he was hit first from behind and was probably un-conscious when he got pounded some more. What do you make of that?"

"What you make of it, I imagine. The

killer either wasn't as mad at Ollie as he was at Harold, or he kept pounding Harold because there wasn't any cliff to toss him off of."

"What do you think of the theory that the killer didn't mean to kill Ollie and tried to make his death look like an accident?"

"I can see that, but whoever killed Harold didn't try to make it look like an accident."

The Chief nodded, then opened a drawer in his desk and brought out an ancient briar. He stuck it in his mouth and chewed on the stem. I eyed the pipe enviously. If I'm ever diagnosed as having an incurable disease I'm going to stoke up again.

"No," said the Chief, "Harold was no accident. The killer wanted him dead. Probably wanted to get it over fast, too, so he could get gone before Maud came home. Which raises another question."

"How he knew Maud would be away from home?"

"Yes. Of course he might not have known. He might have been willing to kill Maud, too, if she'd been at the house. It's possible that Harold got himself killed just because he was in the wrong place at the wrong time. Maybe Ollie got killed for the same reason."

"The idea of these two guys being killed almost by accident is a little hard for me to swallow," I said. "You come up with the murder weapon?"

"No. If you find a bloody club or a bloody piece of two- or three-inch lead pipe I want you to tell me right away."

"You'll be the first to know. You get anything useful out of Maud Mayhew? Harold's enemy list or his hate mail or anything like that?"

"She didn't have any illusions about him even though he was her son. But she was no help when it came to naming anyone who hated him enough to beat him to death. Whoever did it was either a very professional killer or a very angry amateur. There wasn't much left of Harold's skull."

"A professional hit, you think?"

He shook his head. "He wasn't in debt, he wasn't a gambler, he didn't do drugs. We can't come up with any reason a hit man would whack him. I think it was a private matter and that the killer is right here on the island. We're out asking questions and talking to people who might know something, but so far nothing."

And when the police finished talking to everyone, they would start from the beginning and talk to them all again, looking for a break, for a detail someone had neglected to give them before, for a line on someone who had motive and opportunity and a willingness to beat Harold Hobbes's skull into pieces.

They might never find the killer, but murder cases are never closed until someone is convicted of the crime. As far as I knew, the Jack the Ripper case was still open, and this case wouldn't close either, until the killer was nailed, whether or not the Chief and I lived to see it ended in court.

I sat there in the Chief's office, thinking about everything I'd been told, wondering how much of it, if any, consisted of lies and how much of truth, how much meant something and how much meant nothing.

I was looking at a jigsaw puzzle with missing pieces. It was a picture of Martha's Vineyard covered by a spiderweb. Little people, dead and alive, were tangled in the web and linked by its strands one to another. Here and there a missing piece prevented me from seeing a connection. I could see two bodies and a number of living women and men whose names or faces I recognized. In the center of the web was a spider linked unmistakably to the two bodies, but whose human face was on a missing piece.

I searched my memory for those missing pieces, but I couldn't find them.

"This was supposed to be a trade," I said. "I tell you what I know and you tell me what you know."

"In your dreams," said the Chief. "All right, here's something for you: Harold Hobbes had a vasectomy not long before he died. What do you make of that?"

I tried to find a use for that information but failed.

"You have a pained expression," said the Chief. "Tell you what: you leave this murder business to us professionals and you concentrate on catching the Silencer. That way you'll be out of my hair, and, who knows, maybe we'll both get lucky."

"Oh, no, you don't," I said, getting up and heading for the door. "The Silencer is your problem, not mine. If I find out who he is and turn him in, I'll have everybody in the Chamber Music Society and the community chorus on my neck because they like what he's doing. No, you chase him if you must, but leave me out of it. I'm on his side."

"Sure, you are," said the Chief, chomping on his pipe stem. "But will you still feel that way when he decides he doesn't like Beethoven either and melts your *Missa Solemnis*?"

Melt my *Missa Solemnis*?! Maybe the Silencer really was a danger to Western civilization. Maybe I really should stop him while he still had good taste in music.

First, though, I wanted to talk again with Maud Mayhew.

20

I got several chapters of my car book read as I waited in the ferry line to Chappaquiddick and willed another pox upon the Fish and Wildlife people. That week the book was *Prehistoric and Roman Britain,* which had a lot of good pictures.

Maud Mayhew's pickup was parked in front of her house. The place had a vacant feel about it, as though no one had lived there for a while, and I wondered if Maud had gone away.

But she had not. When she answered my knock, though, I saw in her lightless eyes that the vitality that usually animated her was missing, and I realized that it was the lack of this life force that gave the farm its abandoned air. Maud's body was there but her son's death had made it an almost empty shell.

"Come in," she said in an emotionless voice, and she turned and led me into the house. Although the rooms were clean and neat there was no sign of human life in them, no feeling of habitation other than by ghosts.

I wondered if Harold's death was going to kill his mother, if his murderer would be hers as well; or if, as women have done through the ages when their men and children die, she would rally and go on living, tougher and stronger than most men would be if bereft of wife and children.

She waved me to a chair and said, "Would you like some tea?"

"If you're having some."

She nodded and went to the kitchen. While she was gone I looked around the room. There was no dust on the floor and furniture, but I felt like there was. I could feel white sheets covering chairs and sofas.

Maud came back and poured tea into two cups. She sat and looked at me, saying nothing. It had been a week since Harold's murder.

"How are you?" I asked.

"I'm tired."

"Are you getting any sleep?"

She shrugged.

"Your doctor can probably give you something that will help you sleep."

"I don't like pills. Never did."

"Do you have a friend who might come and stay with you for a while?"

Another shrug. "I'd be bad company."

"I want to ask you some questions. I'll come back later if you're too tired."

"I'll be just as tired later, so ask them. They won't make any difference anyhow." Her voice was small and dull.

"All right. Was your second husband related to Alice Hobbes?"

A small nod. "Ben was her brother."

"Were you all friends before you married Ben? You and Ben and Alice?"

She nodded again. "Oh, yes. There were several of us who did things together. Riding, tennis, golf, bridge, sailing, softball. Parties. We palled around a lot."

"You must have been newly divorced about that time."

Her smile was crooked and fleeting. "Free and making the most of it. My first husband was a bore."

"Were the Bradfords and Piersons part of the crowd?"

"Miles Bradford and Sarah Pierson were part of the crowd until they got married and started having children. After that, Sarah dropped out of the circle."

"But not Miles?"

"No," she said, "not Miles. Miles liked

to party and he was good at it."

"He had a bad heart."

"It didn't slow him down."

"It killed him."

Her voice changed tone, losing something of its listlessness. "Yes."

"In Alice Hobbes's bed, I'm told. That must have had an effect on the social swirl."

Her tired eyes studied me. "It ended it. Alice married Pete Mattes. Pete had been after her for years, but he wasn't one of us, and she fended him off until Miles died and she found out she was pregnant. Then she married Pete in a hurry. It was a smart move. They were happy and Pete treated her baby like his own."

I had finally arrived at my true interest. "And you married Ben Hobbes."

She sipped her tea. "Yes."

"And Harold was born a few months later. Less than nine, I think."

"I see that you've been looking at the marriage and birth records."

"No, I thought I should talk to you first."

The wrinkled hand that held her teacup was steady as stone. "Go on, then. Talk. Nothing makes any difference now."

"It might," I said. "I think that Ben was

already wooing you when you discovered that you, like Alice Hobbes, was carrying one of Miles Bradford's children. You accepted Ben's latest proposal, got married, and gave a legal name to Harold."

She drank more tea. "That's about it. Harold had a name and I had another husband I didn't want. I lived with him, though, until he finally drank himself to death. He was a weakling like a lot of men."

"Did he know Harold wasn't his son?"

"He should have suspected. Every woman in our crowd must have known, but men can be blind. Sarah Bradford hasn't spoken to me since, but Ben never mentioned the possibility. When he died I told Harold the truth. I didn't want him thinking that his father was nothing but a sentimental drunk."

I had been seeing through a glass darkly, but now I knew in part. "How did he take the news?" I asked.

"He grew up to be a drunk and a weakling himself. When I married again he began to hurt me with his tongue. When we got divorced, it got worse. What put you onto this ancient history?"

"I saw an old photo of Miles Bradford. It reminded me of someone but it took a

245

while for me to realize that Harold was that person. They were both tall, good-looking men."

She put the cup in its saucer on the low table between us. "And both of them could be charming and both were womanizers. Like father, like son. But what difference does it make now? My son is dead."

"It might have something to do with his murder and with Ollie Mattes's death. It's another link between the two men. They were half brothers. Did Ollie know that?"

"I've never told anyone but Harold who his real father was."

"Maybe Harold told Ollie."

"I doubt it. Ollie Mattes was a leech. He'd have come to me looking for money if he'd known he was related to my son."

"I think you're probably right," I said, remembering what Helga Mattes had told me: that Ollie didn't know Harold and that he had prevailed upon his wife, Helga, to use her cousin's influence to get him the job as watchman at the Pierson house.

She saw something in my face. "Do you think that's significant?"

"I'm not sure." I put my cup beside hers and stood. "I don't think it's good for you to be staying here in the house by yourself. Why don't you get outside? I imagine your garden needs weeding and your animals will need some attention."

She rose. "I'm not suicidal."

"I'm not opposed to rational suicide," I said, "but I don't like to see a useful life end. You own a farm that needs tending and you're not tending it."

She sniffed. "Ten-cent psychology, J.W."

"It's the only brand I handle. For you it's free." I went toward the door. "I'll let you know if I learn anything useful."

She followed me out onto the porch. It was a pleasantly warm day with thin white clouds moving slowly across a pale blue sky.

"It's a good day for gardening," I said, and walked to the Land Cruiser.

She said nothing.

As I pulled away she was still standing in front of the door.

I drove down to the east end of Norton's Point Beach. There was a chain across the entrance to the ORV track we took when the beach was open. A sign advised me that piping plovers were fledging and that vehicles were prohibited.

Not all vehicles, apparently, for down the beach I could see one that probably belonged to the plover police.

During the year before the beach was

first closed, a single plover chick had been found run over by an ORV driven, it was guessed but never proved, by some plover-indifferent fisherman. This was enough evidence for the Fish and Wildlife people to close the beach on the grounds that ORVs were dangerous to plovers. The first year it was closed, another plover chick had been run over by an ORV, this time one definitely driven by a plover protector. The beach stayed closed. The net benefit for plovers: zero.

The plover police vehicle was coming toward me so I waited until it arrived. The driver was a young woman with sun-bleached hair and a good tan. I wondered but didn't ask if she'd squished any plover chicks lately. Instead I smiled my imitation Burt Lancaster smile, told her I was investigating the Chappy murders, and asked if she had noticed any of several vehicles using the beach just before it had closed. I described the vehicles.

"Well, I know that blue Cherokee that Harold Hobbes drove," she said, "but I don't remember the others. A lot of SUVs use this beach."

"Not for most of the summer these days," I said. "Did Harold go back and forth often?"

"Almost every day just before we closed the beach. It was terrible when he got killed. Do they know who did it?"

"Not yet. If you'd noticed these other ORVs it might have narrowed things down a little."

"Sorry," she said. "I'm a biologist, not a police officer. What have those vehicles got to do with anything?"

"The killer either lives on Chappy or got over there somehow, which means he either drove there on this beach or took the On Time. My guess is that he used the beach so no one would know he came and went. I'd hoped you might have seen his SUV."

She was in a devil's advocate mood. "Maybe he had his own boat."

"He could have gotten to Ron Pierson's house by boat, but he'd have had a long walk to get to Maud Mayhew's farm and back again."

"Maybe there were two killers."

"Are you left-handed?"

"No. Why?"

"Because that rules you out as a suspect. Whoever killed Ollie Mattes and Harold Hobbes was a southpaw about your height. The odds are long that there weren't two killers with that same description."

"Why'd he do it? Does anybody know?"

"The killer does."

It was a warm day, but the young woman shivered. Just to be ornery I lost my smile and studied her and said, "Are you sure you're not left-handed?"

She was very sure.

21

Crime never takes a holiday on Martha's Vineyard or anywhere else, and one case is never the only case for the cops. The big cases like the Chappy murders get most of the attention but there are always others, many of which never get into the papers.

I found out about one of these from Gabe Winters at the Newes From America, one of Edgartown's finer pubs, where I'd stopped for a late lunch of amber ale and calamari after talking with Maud Mayhew. Gabe was a cousin of Kit Goulart's and therefore the recipient of all the better crime gossip.

"You're a friend of John Skye's," said Gabe, pausing at my table on his way out. "You hear about the Jaguar in his west pasture?"

"No. The animal or the car?"

"The car. You know those big houses in those new developments south of the West

Tisbury road, down toward the Great Ponds?"

"Yeah."

"Well, it seems that a guy and his wife who live in one of those castles got into an argument that went on until the guy decided to get out of the house and get himself a cup of coffee while things cooled down. So he gets into their Land Rover and starts for Edgartown. But the wife decides she hasn't had enough of him yet so she runs down and gets into their Jaguar and goes after him.

"The cops figure, from the marks on the highway, that she was going about a hundred miles an hour when she comes to that little curve in the road opposite John Skye's pasture. She goes off the road, overcorrects coming back, crosses the road again, goes through John's fence, and rolls the Jag about a dozen times in his pasture, totally demolishing it. The car is upside down and the woman is trapped inside."

"When did this happen?"

"Last week."

"I never heard about it."

"I'm coming to that. The husband sees what happened in his rearview mirror, turns around, and races back. When the cops get there they find him jumping up and down on top of the wrecked car screaming, 'Look what that bitch did to my Jaguar! The bitch ruined my car! Oh, what a bitch!'

"The wife is still trapped in the car, but the cops get her out finally and she's not even hurt bad. The reason you never heard about it is that the next day hubby and wifey are all lovey again and say they never had an argument, that she was only going fifty, not a hundred, that the accident happened because she tried to avoid hitting a dog, that they're paying for a new fence for John Skye, and that it's not worth a news story at all. So it never made the local papers."

"Wild. I imagine the Jag was pretty well insured."

"Probably. You want to know the really funny thing? The car had one of those little computer screens on the dashboard that tells you when something needs attention. You know: 'Your left brake light is out; fix it.' 'Check your oil.' 'Your windshield wiper fluid is low.' Like that. Well, when they get the woman out of this totally destroyed car, that little screen is the only part of it still working, only now it's saying, 'Your engine block is smashed, your axles are broken, your drive shaft is in pieces,

and your tires are all flat.' Funny, huh?"
Gabe was still laughing when he went out
the door.

Another reason to be glad I'd given up
being a cop. There were lots of them.
Someday, I thought, feeling a smile cross
my face, Kit Goulart really should write
her book about being a cop on Martha's
Vineyard. A book like that could probably
be written about every small-town police
force in America.

In fact, Kit could probably write a book
about just this month on the Vineyard,
what with a double murder, the Silencer
zapping sound systems, the adventures of
Mickey Gomes, and this accident, all happening pretty much at once. No wonder
the Chief's hair was gray. He was lucky to
have any at all.

I took my time finishing my ale and
thought about what Maud Mayhew and
others had told me during the last few
days. When the tall glass was empty, it was
time for a second meeting with Ethan
Bradford. I could do that and still be home
before Joshua and Diana got off the school
bus.

Being a parent definitely intruded on my
detecting. No wonder Superman was
single. Even though he was faster than a

speeding bullet, having a wife and kids would have made it hard for him to find time to fight crime and hold down a steady job at the *Daily Planet* too.

As I drove to West Tisbury I didn't envy Superman's bachelor state, but I wouldn't have minded being bulletproof because I vividly remembered Ethan Bradford's shotgun. If he had murdered Ollie Mattes and/or Harold Hobbes, he probably wouldn't be as reluctant as most people would be to put me in the ground.

I wondered if I should have stopped at the house and picked up the old .38 Police Special I'd carried when I'd been a cop in Boston. The problem with having a gun with you is that you might be stressed into using it when you actually didn't have to. The problem with not having one is that you might actually need it. Why hadn't God made a less ambiguous world?

In West Tisbury I turned right onto Old County Road. When I found the side road leading to Ethan's house, I had a last chance to change my mind about seeing him but didn't take it. Instead, I drove to his house. His old Jeep was parked in the yard. I parked beside it and got out.

In the passenger seat of the Jeep was what looked like a box of junk but that might have been some sort of modernistic work of art or an arcane machine. Was Ethan Bradford some sort of sculptor? A guy who manufactured mobiles and static statements out of wires and tubes and other odds and ends from the dump? I'd seen photos of worse-looking stuff in the art pages of the *Globe*.

The door of the house opened before I got halfway there and Bradford stepped out. He held the familiar shotgun in his hand. From the house behind him came the sound of a Vivaldi concerto. I didn't know which one it was, but you can always tell when it's Vivaldi.

"I thought I told you not to come back here," he said in his thin voice. He stepped toward me, but I kept walking. He brought his other hand to the shotgun and swung the weapon across his body, but I didn't stop until I came close to him.

His eyes were the color of his sister's but his face, unlike hers, was tight-skinned and hard. He gripped the shotgun.

"If you're set on shooting," I said, "you'd best get at it. Otherwise put that gun down and stop pretending. I don't have much time to spend here."

I was surprised at how fearless I sounded, but my tone affected him. "What do you want?" he asked.

He still held the shotgun with both hands. I looked at it and said nothing and after a moment he released one hand from it and dropped the muzzle toward the ground.

"Your sister and Harold Hobbes used to come here while they were romancing," I said. "You used to take off while they were here."

"Who told you that crock?"

"Your sister. She said you weren't happy about the relationship. Were you?"

"None of your business."

"The police might think it's theirs. If they find out you didn't like Hobbes but that your sister was in thrall, they might decide that you drove over to his place and smashed his head in. Noble brother to the rescue, like in the old melodramas."

His eyes widened. "Jesus! The last time you were here you thought I killed Ollie Mattes. Now you think I killed Harold Hobbes. You're bound and determined that I killed somebody. Everybody knows that Hobbes was a womanizing bastard, but I didn't kill him."

"Your sister says he'd changed. She says that they were going away together to start a new life."

"My sister is a foolish woman and

Hobbes was a con artist. But she loved him, and she'd never forgive me if I hurt him. I'd have broken them apart if I could have, but I couldn't because of her. I didn't cry a tear when I heard he was dead, but I didn't kill him. I've never killed anybody in my life!"

I nodded at the shotgun. "You threatened me with that."

He clutched the shotgun. "I never did. You may have thought I did, but I didn't." He broke the gun open. "Look. It's not loaded. It wasn't loaded then, either."

I gestured at the sagging house and barn. "You live like a wild man, like one of those militia types out in Idaho. It's easy to think you'd kill somebody without too much thought. Hobbes was a natural target for you."

"Yeah? Well, I didn't kill him. I can prove it. I was someplace else that night."

"Where?"

He became careful. "None of your business."

"You have witnesses?"

"I can prove where I was." The care in his voice was colored with confidence. I changed tack.

"Who hated Harold Hobbes enough to kill him?"

258

"How about half the women on this island?"

"Your sister says it was getting hard for you to keep her secret. Who'd you tell?"

"Nobody. I told nobody."

But a quaver in his voice said differently.

"You're a poor liar," I said. "When the cops get you in an interrogation room, they'll get the truth out of you fast enough. Save yourself some pain."

Vivaldi's violins danced over us as he tried to decide what to do. Finally he leaned forward and said, "I didn't tell anybody but my mother. I wanted to break them up but I didn't want to be the one to do it. I knew my mom could. She's done it before. She hates men and I knew she'd take Cheryl away from him."

I had no sympathy for him. "I understand you're one of the men she doesn't like. Does she like you better now?"

His voice was so forlorn that my feelings unexpectedly reversed themselves and I felt compassion for him. "I wanted her to, but I don't know. I hope she does. She had a hard time with my father. She thinks all men are like him. But they're not. I'm not like him. I wish she knew that."

I couldn't grant him that wish and the school bus would soon be stopping at the

259

end of our driveway, so I left him there with Vivaldi and drove home, feeling almost light-headed as I thought about what I knew.

22

"Look at this, Pa." Joshua was having his turn on the computer. I looked. On the screen was a document about microwaves.

"Are you learning how to cook?" I asked.

"No. We're doing this peace project at school," said my son, "and one of the parts is about how to have a war without killing anybody so I'm finding out stuff about that."

I hadn't expected summer school mostly about nature studies to include subjects like that, but why shouldn't it? Maybe naturalists could come up with a better way to have wars.

"I read once about some people up in the Arctic who fought their wars by facing off and yelling insults at each other," I said. "The best insulters won the war and nobody ever got hurt."

"I'll put that in my report, but I'm going to put this in too. Look, it says right there that high-powered microwaves can make somebody unconscious without doing any permanent damage to them. You shoot them with your high-powered microwave gun and they're knocked out and you capture them and when they wake up they're your prisoner. Neat!"

Neat indeed. "Do they actually have guns like that?"

"I don't know if they have any that work yet, but it says here that they're doing experiments with them and with other kinds of microwave weapons, too." He scrolled down the page. "See there? They're making ones that will stop a tank or an airplane or a rocket or a cannon from working. The microwaves stop their motors, and the machines won't work." He smiled up at me. "That's pretty good if you want a war where nobody gets hurt. You just stop their soldiers and their machines with your microwaves."

I put my hands on his shoulders. "If you ever have to go to war, I hope it's that kind, but it's better not to have one at all."

"Yeah, peace is best, but a microwave war would be better than the other kind. I'm going to say that in my paper."

"Good." Plato, who thought that only the dead had seen the end of war, would surely agree one without blood and gore would be an improvement.

"Pa?"

"What?"

"I'm going to say that if you'd been in a microwave war you wouldn't have all those scars on your legs. Is that okay?"

"A lot of soldiers got hurt worse than I did, Joshua."

"I know, but I think it will be good if I can show how people right here on Martha's Vineyard would be safer if they only had microwave wars."

"Put me in, then. You can say that I got wounded by shrapnel from a shell that killed some of the soldiers I was with, but that if we'd been in a microwave war, maybe no one would have been hurt."

I suspected that most wars would continue to be fought the bloody, old-fashioned way and doubted that the gunner who had fired that fatal shell at my companions and me had ever heard of microwaves.

Until my talk with Joshua I had known about microwave ovens but had otherwise not been much better educated about electrical energy than that Vietnamese gunner. But Joshua had turned a light on inside my brain and I had that rush of happy certainty that comes when you suddenly see how to win a chess game in five moves or solve a puzzle that up till now totally eluded you. From the mouths of babes.

"Pa?"

"What?"

"How do you spell 'shrapnel'?"

I told him how to spell it and what it was. I didn't tell him that even now, decades after I'd been hit, small pieces of metal still occasionally worked their way out through the skin of my calves, causing sores that continued to keep me from a profitable career as a Bermuda shorts model.

When the kids were in bed, Zee played adviser-if-needed as I took my turn at the computer and found my way single-handedly to the Internet, where I brought up pages and pages of information about electronic warfare. Most of it required slow reading, but I had time and Zee showed me how to print out the material I wanted to study most. It was late when we went to bed.

"You're wearing your thoughtful look," said Zee, as we lay in bed with our books. "What's on your mind?"

"Your body." I took a hand off my book and slid it under the blanket.

"No tickling! What, really?"

"A moral dilemma. What to do if I know who the Silencer is and how he does his work."

"Give him a medal?"

"That's one possibility. He's improving the island as far as I'm concerned."

"Do you really think you know who it is?"

"I think I know who it could be. I'll have to ask to be sure."

She put a hand under the blanket and captured mine. "What if you don't ask? What if you just let nature take its course?"

"Like what? Letting him keep on destroying thousands of dollars' worth of sound equipment until he grows old and dies of natural causes sometime in the next hundred years?"

"Why not?"

"It's tempting. But the Chief asked me how I'd feel if the Silencer started silencing the music I like."

Zee knew the answer to that one: "Silence Beethoven? Pavarotti? Vince Gill? No problem if that happens. Lock him up for life."

I dropped my book onto the floor and got my other hand to work beneath the covers. "I love a decisive woman," I said. "I can't resist one when I find her in my bed."

"You probably couldn't resist a porcupine in heat," said Zee, dropping her own book and turning toward me. "As for me, I like a man with slow hands."

"You're in luck," I said. "All truly manly men have slow hands and there's no man more truly manly than me."

"Show me," she said. "I have time."

I did that and forgot about the Silencer.

The next morning I phoned Quinn, up in Boston. He wasn't at his desk at the *Globe*, so I left a message. I wondered how many times I'd driven up-island in the last week and decided to spare myself another trip if possible by making another phone call, this one to Cheryl Bradford.

The voice that answered belonged to her mother, Sarah. I gave her my name, reminded her of our brief meeting a few days before, and added that I'd had the pleasure of seeing her hit a homer in the codger game.

Her voice was not cordial. "Oh? Are you following both me and my daughter around now, Mr. Jackson?"

"No, but I might give it some thought if I wasn't already a happily married man. I was at the game for another reason."

"To talk with Kristen Kolle. I saw the two of you together. Do you socialize with any men, or just with women?"

"It wasn't a social conversation. Is your daughter home?"

"Cheryl isn't available right now, Mr. Jackson. She's still recovering from a death in the family."

"I have a question to ask her. Just one. I won't take more than a moment of her time."

"Sorry, Mr. Jackson. Please don't call again." The phone clicked in my ear.

So much for saving another trip up-island. I got into the truck and drove to the Bradford place in Chilmark. Both Sarah's SUV and Cheryl's Volvo were in the yard. I parked between them and went to the door of the house.

Sarah Bradford, her face filled with anger, opened it. Her voice was as cold as her face was hot.

"I told you not to call. I meant it. Go away and don't come back, or I'll call the police and charge you with stalking my daughter!"

"I want to speak with Cheryl," I said. "She's a grown woman who doesn't need any protection from you."

"She's a fool who knows nothing about

267

men, including you! Get out!"

"I want to see her." I was a foot taller than she was, and threw my voice over her head into the house. "Cheryl! It's J. W. Jackson! I want to ask you a question!"

"I'm calling the police!" Sarah stepped back and tried to slam the door, but I stopped it with my foot. She pushed on the door and I saw her daughter come into the room behind her. Her mother spun to follow my gaze. "Go back to your room!" she snapped.

"Just one question," I said to Cheryl, and she took a deep breath and came across the room. Her mother released the door and ran like a deer into the house.

"What is it?" said Cheryl. "What do you want to know?"

In a quiet voice, I said, "Just one thing: Did your mother insist that you break off your relationship with Harold Hobbes when she found out about it?"

She looked bewildered, then gave a quick glance behind her and stepped out onto the porch, closing the door behind her. "No," she whispered. "Of course she didn't. She didn't know about us. And I don't want her to know! Please don't tell her! If she knew, she'd be livid. You saw just now how angry she can be. You'd better go. I think she really is calling the police."

"If they show up, I'd appreciate it if you tell them that I'm not stalking you."

"I will. But you'd better go."

I agreed with her and left.

At home I called Quinn again and this time he answered. "You should get yourself an answering machine," he said. "I called you twice and nobody was home."

"That's why I don't have one," I said. "I don't want to get endless messages from you. All I want to know is whether you found out anything about Ethan Bradford and Connell Aerospace."

"The Fourth Estate has a long reach," said Quinn. "I talked with a couple of the people I met when I did that earlier story. Seems like a prototype weapon Connell was developing went missing and hasn't been seen since. Bradford had been working on it. He was the prime suspect but they couldn't prove he was involved in its disappearance so they couldn't charge him. But they could fire him and they did."

"What was the weapon?"

"They were very coy about the details, but apparently it was some sort of portable electronic device. Something small enough for one man to carry around. Shoots microwaves of some kind. The military is big on microwave weapons these days, apparently. I can probably find out more about it if it's important. What's going on?"

"Did the theft set the program back enough to cost the company a lot of money?"

"I wondered the same thing. I guess it wasn't the only model they had, and apparently it was still in an experimental stage and didn't really work well. What worried Connell was that whoever stole it might sell it to another country or to another company that might bring it out first. If that happened, Connell could lose millions in military contracts. Are you going to tell me what this is all about, or not?"

"Not. At least not now. I'll pay you in bluefish if you ever stop muckraking long enough to come down and go fishing."

"I know Zee would like that," said Quinn. "She could stand some sophisticated company for a change."

"I think you've got sophism and sophistication mixed up," I said, "but come down anyway."

I hung up before he could get in a last one-liner.

23

Our normal obligations do not cease simply because crime has intruded upon our lives. No matter what, as the poet noted, we're gonna come and we're gonna go and somebody's got to pay the rent.

So I took a bottle of Sam Adams outside under the warm early-summer sky and worked in the garden while I thought things over. There were enough pea pods to make a meal, so I picked those and then did some weeding and watering. Soon the lawn would need mowing, and I would be pushing around the perfectly good lawn mower I'd salvaged from the dump years before, when it was The Big D, the island's favorite secondhand store. In those golden days you could find lots of good stuff there and return whatever you didn't want to keep, no questions asked, and the environmentalists had not yet persuaded the authorities that dumps were bad and should be eliminated.

Maybe I should get some goats to keep the grass trim. How did people keep their lawns trimmed before they had lawn mowers? The owners of those stately mansions in England, for instance; how did they do it?

Or did they do it? Maybe they didn't have lawns, or maybe they didn't keep them trimmed. Maybe I could find out by looking up "lawns" on the Internet. Maybe somebody had written a History of Lawns in which were answers to all my questions and more.

Boldly I abandoned my garden and went to the computer, where, all alone, I reached the Web and looked up "lawns" and found out that, indeed, books had been written on the subject. In practically no time I learned that the word "lawn," meaning maintained turf, had appeared in the 1500s, that grass lawns had become important in the 1700s and had been cut by scythes (three men could cut an acre a day), and that mechanized lawn mowers had been developed in the 1800s.

Amazing. Maybe having the computer was as good a thing as the rest of my family and the world thought it was! I now knew more about lawns than I'd ever known before.

Too bad the computer couldn't tell me if all my brooding and guessing were actually pointing me toward the killer who had coshed Ollie Mattes and Harold Hobbes.

Garbage in, garbage out. Wasn't that what the techie people said? If you put wrong information into your computer, you'll get wrong information out.

My problem was that I wasn't sure what was garbage and what wasn't, so even if I could feed my computer everything I knew or thought I knew, which I couldn't, it still wouldn't give me the answer I sought.

We live in an imperfect world.

Or maybe in a perfect one we just don't understand.

Such profundity. It was my specialty du jour.

I had another beer with lunch while listening to the noon news on our radio. Nothing had changed. If I went to Mars for ten years and came back and turned on the noon news, would anything have changed? Not a lot, probably. Was that heartening or disheartening?

I put on my tape of *La Traviata*, featuring fellow islander Beverly Sills as Violetta. Then, as I sipped a third Sam Adams and prepared chicken and snow peas for supper, I listened, eyes full of tears, as Violetta, doomed but worthy of immortal love, poured out her songs to me alone. Oh, Beverly, oh, Violetta, we could have had such a damned good time together!

When the preparations for the evening meal were complete and poor Violetta had, alas, expired once again, I studied the printouts I had taken from the Internet the evening before.

The only ones I could begin to understand were the papers written by experts for know-nothings like me. There were many such papers, evidence that there were a lot more know-nothings than experts in the world, but that the know-nothings, military ones in this case, had the money the experts needed to practice their expertise.

The microwave experts presenting these papers were explaining to the know-nothings what they were working on in the way of electronic weapons, and why. In order to do this, they used the jargon of their science, and I and the other know-nothings had to understand it. If I read slowly I could keep track of at least some of the explanations and the initials that referred to key terms.

Radio frequency (RF) weapons technology was the subject, and apparently a lot of countries, the Soviet Union especially, were or had been involved in developing such weapons. Many were experimenting with directed energy weapon systems, pulsed power technologies, high power microwave (HPM) technologies, particle beams, and related subjects I could not pretend to understand technically.

The significant point seemed to be that RF weapons might be used against all sorts of targets, including land mines, missiles, and communication systems, to say nothing of the plain human beings to whom Joshua had drawn my attention.

A paradox, duly noted by the experts, was that the USA, by dint of being a highly technically developed nation, was thus more vulnerable to RF attack than were less-developed nations. As always with science, yang was balanced by yin. I should probably hang on to my straight-blade knives, just in case.

One of the problems with RF weapons was their size and their need for a potent power source, but as research continued, the prospect of a portable HPM weapon was becoming more feasible. Experiments with solid-state pulsers and high-current electronic accelerators (What were they? Never mind) suggested that briefcase-sized devices weighing only a few pounds were feasible. All your RF shootist would need to blast his target would be a directional antenna to project his HPM.

Manny Fonseca, the Vineyard's foremost pistoleer and Zee's shooting instructor, would be fascinated.

The general point of the papers was that there was more and more RF equipment capable of disrupting electronic systems, and that the United States needed to develop such weapons and simultaneously develop defenses against them. I suspected that the military would find the money to do just that. More of my tax dollars at work.

I put my papers away and drove to the police station in Edgartown. There was a state police cruiser in the parking lot. Inside the station, Kit Goulart was again at the front desk, and the Chief's office door was closed.

"J.W., you should join the force," she said. "That way you'd get paid for spending all your time here."

"No thanks. I was a cop once and once was enough." I jabbed a thumb toward the closed door. "I presume that the Chief and

276

Dom Agganis are conferring. Any chance of breaking in on the cabal?"

"I can but inquire," said Kit. "Do you have a good reason why the high priests should allow you to enter the inner sanctum?"

"The weed of crime and its bitter fruit."

"Oh. I don't know if that will do it, but I'll pass your metaphor along."

"It's all I have to offer, I'm afraid."

She picked up a phone and spoke into it, listened, and hung up. "Have a seat. The Chief will be free in just a few minutes. How's the family?"

"The family has entered the computer age," I said, and told her of our purchase. "Zee and the kids are all better at using it than I am, but I'm improving."

"Well, someone had to be the last person in America to own one," said Kit, "and it's no surprise that it was you."

"I'm still getting used to internal combustion engines," I said. "It's tough for me to deal with newfangled stuff like electricity."

The Chief opened the door of his office and waved me in. Dom Agganis was seated in one of the hard chairs in front of the Chief's desk. He nodded to me as the

Chief sat down behind his desk. His chair was padded.

"What can I do for you, J.W.?"

"How about telling me who killed Ollie Mattes and Harold Hobbes."

"No comment. Do you know?"

"Not yet. Do you have a list of the dates when the Silencer did his work?"

"Why do you want to know?" The Chief and Dom exchanged tired looks.

"It might help me figure out who he is. You gave me that job, remember?"

"I didn't give you the job. I just wanted you out from under our feet. My plan obviously didn't work."

"Maybe not, but I think I know how the Silencer does his work, at least."

"Oh? How?"

I told them about microwave weapons. "I think he fries sound systems with HPM radio frequencies," I concluded.

Dom and the Chief again exchanged looks. "How'd you come up with this notion?" asked Dom.

I told them. They expressed amused amazement. "Sounds good," said Dom to the Chief. "We can round up the usual suspects and eliminate everybody who doesn't own a microwave weapon."

I said, "If I knew when the Silencer did

his work, I might be able to narrow the list of candidates."

The Chief studied me. "You know something you're not telling us. What is it?"

"Your suspicions injure me deeply. Can I have the list of dates?"

He thought about it, then went to a file cabinet and got out a folder. "Most of this information's been in the papers, so it's no secret," he said. He went to the door and said, "Kit, will you make a copy of this file for me? Thanks."

She did and brought it to him. He leafed through it and extracted a few pages he didn't think were any of my business then handed the others to me. They were reports about police responses to angry citizens complaining about disabled sound systems in their cars and homes.

"If you zero in on this guy, let me know," said the Chief.

"You can trust me," I said, heading for the door.

"Sure I can," said the Chief.

24

At home I studied the papers the Chief had given me. Most of the dates meant nothing to me, but two did. I got on the phone and called Cheryl Bradford, figuring I had an even chance of getting her instead of her mother. I was wrong; I got their answering machine. I hung up without leaving a message.

Everybody in the world but me had an answering machine, and my friends and family had long thought that I should get one too. Maybe so. After all, we already had a cell phone, and now that I'd belatedly entered the computer age, maybe I should go another short step into the twenty-first century. Buck Rogers would be flying around with Wilma in only another four hundred years. Time was zipping by.

I considered and then rejected the idea of phoning Ethan Bradford, because I had just enough time to make another drive to his place and I wanted to have a look at his Jeep. I'd spent so much time up-island in the last few days that pretty soon Chilmark and West Tisbury were going to want me to pay residency taxes.

Were there such things as residency taxes? If not, there probably soon would be, and Chilmark, ever on the alert to the danger of poor people living there, would be among the first to impose them.

I was pleased to see Ethan's old Jeep parked in his yard. I parked beside it, got out, and studied the contraption in the passenger seat. It looked less like modern sculpture to me this time, and more like something Rube Goldberg might have built.

But it wasn't a piece of junk. Even though I had no idea about exactly what its wires and attached devices were intended to do, there was an unmistakable orderliness to its construction. It was the size of a suitcase, and down there on the floor was what looked to me like an antenna of some sort.

I heard the sound of Baroque music and looked up. Ethan Bradford, shotgun in hand, stood in the open door. His expression was, as usual, angry, but it was also wary and questioning.

"What do you want this time? Am I

going to have to put up a locked gate to keep you away from here?"

"This may be my last visit," I said. "Do you meet everyone with that shotgun in your hand?"

He looked at the gun, then leaned it against the wall. "It discourages most people. When I want company I invite it. I don't want it the rest of the time."

"Do you have a lot of uninvited people coming down here?"

"Not a lot. You're the first one who's come back. What do you want?"

I pointed a finger at the machine in his Jeep. "Would you like to tell me what this gadget is?"

He rubbed his chin. "It's a pile of junk."

"No, it isn't. You're an electrical engineer. It's a machine."

His eyes became careful. "It's a pile of crap I'm taking to the dump. You want to come along?"

"Sure. I'd like to watch you throw this away."

He stayed at the door, eyeing me. "You an electrician?"

"No, but I can read."

"You a cop of some kind? You working for somebody?"

"Like who?"

"Like Connell Aerospace. Don't they have anything better to do than stay on my back? I've been gone from them for over a year."

"I don't work for Connell, but I know something about you getting through there. This gadget left with you, they say."

"To hell with them."

I leaned against the Jeep and crossed my arms. "Let me tell you what I think. I think this machine is a portable HPM weapon. You were working on some kind of an RF weapon when you were at Connell, and when the prototype disappeared you got through. They thought you stole it, but couldn't prove it. I think they were right. I think you brought it here and that you use it to melt sound systems blasting music you don't like. I think you're the Silencer."

There was a Silencer-worthy silence while we eyed each other.

I went on. "You don't like the way technology is being used these days and you're a Baroque music man. Vivaldi, Bach, Telemann, and those guys. You hate the crap that passes for modern music and the sound systems that fill the air with it. To you, it's noise pollution. So you drive around like Robin Hood and fry the electronic systems that boom it from cars and from houses where people are partying. You do it with microwaves or electronic pulses or whatever you call them."

More silence.

"For what it's worth," I said, "I agree with your view of that noise that passes for modern music. And I think the island's better off without those cars with the sound wound up and windows wound down, and houses bouncing off their foundations and neighbors being deafened."

"I didn't steal anything from Connell," said Bradford. "I designed this machine and if I don't own it, who does?"

"Connell thinks it does and they probably have a battalion of lawyers who can make their case."

"Fuck them and their lawyers too. Their prototype didn't even work when I left Connell. I personally built this machine. Connell has other prototypes but I'll give you odds that they haven't solved the power problem yet. They're probably still fooling around with compact explosives. All the power I need I get from my car's cigarette lighter. That would raise a few eyebrows at Connell, you can be damned sure."

There was pride in his voice.

"So it is an HPM weapon," I said.

His smile was a sneer. "You'll never prove it. While you're off rounding up cops to arrest me, I can take it apart and you won't find anybody who can put it together again."

"That would be quite a sacrifice," I said. "You can probably patent this design and sell it back to Connell for a fortune. They'll do a lot of forgiving for a portable RF weapon that works."

He shook his head. "A fortune won't do me any good if I sell this to Connell and then they decide to charge me with theft, or you convince the local cops that I'm the Silencer and I end up in jail. Besides, I already have a trust fund. I don't need any more money than I have."

"I haven't said anything about talking with the cops, and I think you can have a contract written that'll keep Connell from double-crossing you. Brady Coyne is a smart lawyer up in Boston and he's a friend of mine. He can write a contract that God couldn't break. What did you do to get yourself fired from Connell?"

His voice grew hard. "Nothing! That bastard Ron Pierson found out I was working there and canned me. Didn't want his labs polluted by the likes of me. My side of the family is trash as far as he's concerned. The Piersons have a long memory for slights."

"He hired Ollie Mattes to guard his house, and Ollie's kin of his, just like you."

"I hear Ron's wife put the squeeze on him to hire Ollie. Nobody did that for me. Besides, Ollie was working a slave shift and I was an engineer. Ron probably figured I hate his family as much as he hates mine and that I'd sooner or later rip him off. So he fired me."

"And he was right. You did rip him off."

"Like hell. Like I said, I built this machine. It's mine."

There are no feuds like family feuds. "Your mother is a Pierson," I said. "Maybe it's more of that Pierson hate that accounts for her attitude toward men. Other women have had philandering husbands, but most of them don't become man-haters."

"Maybe not, but you leave my mother out of this."

I studied him, wondering if I was reading him right. Just because his shotgun had been unloaded before didn't mean it was unloaded today. I felt a little hollow spot in my belly when I spoke.

"You didn't like Harold Hobbes and after you got fired you had good reason not to like Ron Pierson. If the cops find that out, it'll put you pretty high on their list of murder suspects. They'll figure you knocked off Harold because you didn't want him hanging around with your sister and that you knocked off Ollie Mattes when he tried to stop you from maybe torching Pierson's house."

He opened his mouth but I held up an open hand and stopped his voice. "When we talked before, you said you could prove you were someplace else the evening Harold Hobbes was killed. How about the night Ollie was killed? Can you prove you were somewhere else then, too?"

His eyes widened. "I didn't kill anybody! I didn't even know those guys were dead until they died. I was in Oak Bluffs both nights. I can prove it!"

"How?"

He hesitated, but the possibility of a murder charge was a far stronger threat than was a confession to lesser crimes. "Both times I was zapping boom boxes in OB! Both times! They can nail me for that, but they damned well can't nail me for murder!"

"The only way you can make that alibi stand up is to give the cops details that never got into the papers."

"I can do that. I will do that. Jesus, you

287

don't let up, do you? You can't nail me for one thing, you'll nail me for another. What is it with you?"

I was trying to decide what to believe. As usual there was no way of knowing absolutely, and I had to make a leap of faith one way or another. Leaps of faith, if made sincerely, can lead to total conviction, which is a nice feeling that I distrust. I made my leap anyway but subtracted the pleasure of complete faith in my decision.

"It's nothing to me," I said. "I don't plan to tell the police anything. I already checked the dates the Silencer was active, and he was active in Oak Bluffs the nights of the two murders, just like you say you were. You couldn't have been in OB and on Chappy at the same time, so you're in the clear as far as I'm concerned."

"I can prove that without any help from you."

"Yeah, but then the cops can nail you for being the Silencer and that could put you away for a while, because you've burned out some very, very expensive equipment owned by some very, very mad people."

A hard smile crossed his face. "If you don't tell 'em, I won't."

I returned the same sort of smile. "If I don't and you don't, the Silencer can just keep up his work until someday he makes a slip and gets caught. I don't like the idea of that happening, but I also don't like the idea of dropping a dime on him. So here's what I think should happen. I think the Silencer should retire undefeated, untied, and unscored upon. I think he should return to the darkness whence he came. It will be a while before the noisemakers realize he's gone, so we'll get at least one quiet summer because of him. What do you think?"

His smile warmed a degree or two. "I really hate that din that they call music. It wouldn't be so bad if they just kept it turned down and closed their windows, but —"

"I couldn't agree more, but —"

"I think I made the world better, and I had a lot of fun."

"And you gave a lot of people peace and quiet. You were the Zorro of the island music scene."

"All right," he said. "The Silencer has retired."

"He'll be missed, but I think it's for the best."

"Maybe I *will* contact Connell."

"Why don't you get in touch with Brady Coyne first? He can give you good advice about what to do and how to do it."

I found a scrap of paper in my glove compartment and scribbled Brady's name and phone number on it. "Tell him I sent you to him," I said, handing Ethan the paper. "Be absolutely straight with him, and he'll give you good advice. Take it."

"Thanks."

I pointed at the shotgun. "And don't wave that at people anymore. It's illegal and someone might call the cops."

"It's not loaded."

"It doesn't make any difference."

He took a deep breath. "All right. No more shotgun."

I drove away wondering if I'd made the right decisions regarding Ethan and if I was right in my near conviction about who had killed Harold Hobbes and Ollie Mattes, and why.

25

The next morning as I cleared and washed the breakfast dishes I was aware that time sequences were eluding me, that I could not remember clearly when certain things had happened. When the last plate was stacked in the drain, I phoned Kristen Kolle. Her son answered the phone and told me where she worked: at a real estate office in Edgartown. I drove down to talk with her.

The firm where Kristen Kolle worked was just off Main Street, and since it was still fairly early in the day, I actually managed to find a parking place within walking distance.

Kristen was seated at a desk to my right when I came through her door. She smiled a realtor's smile before she recognized me, and kept it on afterward. One of the reasons I'd be a flop as a realtor or any other kind of salesperson is that I can't smile long enough to convince strangers that I'm their friend.

"Mr. Jackson. How nice to see you again. What can I do for you?"

"You can refresh my memory. Do the ladies who play the codger game play the same day every week or does the day vary?"

"Every Tuesday afternoon, weather permitting, for about ten weeks during the summer. Mom wouldn't miss it."

"Do they always play in the same place?"

"Yes. Right there where you saw them playing earlier this week. The league arranges for a man to keep the field mowed and raked but the players do everything else themselves: putting down the bases, maintaining the backstop and benches, and all that sort of thing."

"How long do the games usually last?"

"It depends. They're usually over by five, but every now and then there's an extra-inning game that goes longer."

"Good exercise. Any extra-inning games lately?"

"Not so far this year, but the season is young."

"Can anyone play?"

"They're mostly regulars but I think anyone who's the right sex and age can probably get on a team. You don't qualify on either count."

"And you're too young. Who provides the bats, balls, and gloves?"

"The league buys the balls, but it's every woman for herself when it comes to bats and gloves. Every team buys its own caps. You don't need a uniform, but you need a cap so people will know whether you're friend or enemy that day."

"Ya can't tell the players without a program. They lose much equipment?"

"Every now and then a ball gets lost in the pucker brush, but that doesn't happen too often. If you break your bat, you borrow one until you can buy yourself a new one. It doesn't take much equipment to have fun playing softball."

That was true of most good games; they were cheap. Poor kids played stickball or shot rubber balls at a fruit basket hung on a wall or kicked a tin can around. You should be wary of games that cost a lot of money.

"And when the game's over everybody goes home?"

"Mostly. Sometimes a few friends get together for cocktails before they head for the shower. Why are you so interested in the codger game?"

"My time line is fuzzy. I'm trying to clear it up. How are sales these days?"

"Good but never good enough. It's the curse of the real estate business. You don't want to sell your place and buy another one, do you?"

"No."

"I understand that you've got fifteen acres of land up there in Ocean Heights. Fifteen acres on Martha's Vineyard, especially when some of it has an ocean view, is worth a lot."

"My father bought it cheap when the area was considered the boondocks and nobody else wanted it. If I get desperate for money I'll let you know."

"You could sell a building lot or two and still have most of it for yourself."

"Right now I've got all of it for myself."

"Well, if you change your mind I do hope you'll give me the first shot at selling it."

She had never lost the smile that had appeared when I'd come through the door. I gave one back to her and left.

I walked to the town offices and found out who was on the Parks and Recreation Department, then made three phone calls before I found a department member at home. Fortunately for me, she actually knew what I wanted to know: that the plover-defending biologist who'd spoken to me down at Norton's Point Beach went on duty at 8 a.m. and left at 5 p.m., just like a person with a normal, legitimate job. I asked if the biologist had been at work before the beach had been closed and was told that she had been on the job since spring.

I thanked my informant for her help and walked down Main, intending to go to the Dock Street Coffee Shop. A police cruiser was parked in front of the hardware store and when I got to the four corners, I found the Chief standing by the bank overseeing a young summer cop who was practicing directing traffic before very many cars were actually on the street. I thought the young cop was doing pretty well and said so.

"So far," said the Chief. "We'll see how she does when the tourists wake up and come downtown."

"I have some news for you," I said. "My sources tell me that the Silencer has decided to retire."

The Chief gave me a cool stare. "Is that a fact? Who are your sources?"

"They prefer to remain anonymous."

"How anonymous will they be if I stick you in front of a judge?"

"I'll be glad to testify under oath, but I should tell you that I've already forgotten this conversation."

The Chief was watching his summer cop again. "I never have much confidence in anonymous sources or high-level spokespersons who decline to be identified."

"In this case the proof will be in the pudding. If more sound systems get melted, you'll know my sources were wrong. If they stop getting fried, you'll know they were right."

"I hope they're right," said the Chief. "My oldest grandchildren love that ear-busting hard rock and hip-hop or whatever they call it, but I hate it. It gives me a headache. Why don't people listen to Harry James anymore?"

I didn't know and said so before going on down to the Dock Street, where I worked my way through a cup of coffee and a bagel while I stacked ideas into various configurations.

Across the parking lot, the Yacht Club's lately rebuilt wing looked shiny and new in contrast to the weathered shingle exterior of the rest of the building.

Yachting was an exception to the rule that good games were cheap. Zee and I owned a catboat but I doubted if the

Shirley J qualified as a yacht or that I could be thought of as a yachtsman. If I could, why hadn't I been invited to join the Yacht Club? After all, unlike some members, we actually had a boat. Maybe if I wore socks with my boat shoes I'd catch the eye of the membership committee.

Probably not.

I could have used more thinking time, but the dreaded meter maids and men were already abroad in the streets of Edgartown and would soon be zeroing in on my truck, so I finished my food, walked to the truck, and drove it to a new location. Then I walked back to the Chief.

"You again. What is it this time?"

"Anything new in the murder investigation?"

"Nothing since the last time you asked me that question, but we're still on the job and we'll find the perp eventually. I don't suppose your anonymous sources know who done it and can save us some time."

"I'm not sure what the anonymous sources know, but I can tell you what I've been doing and what I think."

"You already told me some of your life story."

"There's more."

The Chief looked up and down the

street the way cops do without thinking about it, then put his back against the wall of the bank and his eyes back on the summer cop. "Go ahead."

I leaned on the bricks beside him and told him almost everything about the people I'd seen and what I'd observed or heard. I didn't tell him about the HPM device I'd spotted and the Silencer conversation I'd had with Ethan Bradford. I don't tell anybody everything.

When I was through we were both silent for a while.

"I don't know," he said finally. "You could be right, but it's mostly guesswork. The pieces seem to fit, but a good defense lawyer could probably make mincemeat of the case. It's too circumstantial. It could mean nothing. The D.A. isn't about to go to court just to look like a fool."

"It's not all circumstantial."

"I don't trust your ten-cent psychology, either. We'd have our shrink swearing to one thing and they'd have their shrink swearing just the opposite."

He was right about that. Dueling psychiatrists were common sights in court cases, which was evidence to me that their profession was a dubious one at best.

I said, "There's also motive and opportunity and a weapon."

"There's no weapon."

"There's an implied weapon."

"Implied isn't good enough and you know it. We need one with bloodstains."

We were again quiet for a time. Then I said, "Wire me and maybe I can get a confession."

"And maybe you can't. Maybe all you'll do is spook the quarry. Or maybe you'll get your head smashed in like Mattes and Hobbes."

"Ollie and Harold weren't expecting trouble. I will be. My head will be fine."

"No," said the Chief. "It's too chancy. Go home and leave this to us. You've done enough already. We'll take it from here."

"I think you should wire me."

"No. Now go home and stay there. Weed your garden or mow the lawn or something while I get in touch with Dom Agganis."

He walked toward the cruiser.

How did he know my lawn needed mowing?

I watched the summer cop for a while, then I went to my truck and drove to Vineyard Electronics in Vineyard Haven, where I bought a small battery-powered tape recorder.

26

"Ah, Vanity," said the dying but ever ironic
Cyrano, "I knew you'd overthrow me in the
end." I was familiar with vanity. Mine said
that I was the one to finish what I'd started,
so for what seemed like the millionth time I
drove up-island.

The tape recorder was duct-taped to my
ribs, under my left arm; its mike was taped
to my chest, about level with the mouth of
a medium-sized person. I could turn the
recorder on by casually crossing my arms
and touching a switch.

The Chief thought my plan could be
dangerous, but vanity said that all I had to
do was be careful. I even enjoyed feeling a
little nervous, thinking that it was good to
feel that way because it would make me
more alert.

It was another lovely island day, with a
warm sun and high, thin clouds making
the sky a pale blue. As I turned down the

Bradford driveway I could see the fenced green fields reaching down to the marshes, beyond which the blue ocean lapped at the yellow sand. Emerald and gold and sapphire. Vineyard colors. There were horses in the fields, and outside the pasture fences forests swayed gently in a soft southwest wind.

Cheryl's and Sarah's cars were in the yard. I parked between them and took a minute to examine Sarah's SUV. There was sand inside the rear bumper and under the fenders. I walked to the house, where Cheryl answered my knock. I told her I wanted to speak with her mother. She pointed to the barn.

"She's there. She's just come in from a ride."

"How's she feeling?"

Cheryl made a small gesture with her hands. "She has good days and bad ones. Lately there have been more bad days. She has medication for the pain but it doesn't always do the job. But she won't stop living her life. She has a will of iron."

"She can whack a softball a long way."

"They say she'll be strong right up to the last. When her time comes, it will come fast. One day she'll be here and the next she won't. She knows it and she has no self-pity. I'm not as strong." She paused and looked at me with eyes as innocent as a child. "I just wish she was the kind of person who'd led a happy life, but she isn't and she never was, not even before this sickness. And now it's too late for her. Don't you think you should be happy whenever you can?"

"Yes."

"She's never been unhappy, she's just never been happy."

Anhedonia may not be as rare as we think. "For some people being happy is a risk they don't want to take," I said.

"It's one I'll take. I'm not happy now but I've been happy and I want to be happy again. I hope I will be." She rubbed a hand across her mouth and brushed her fingers under her eyes.

"I hope so too," I said.

"Why do you want to see my mother?"

"I just want to ask her a couple of questions. It won't take long."

"I'll go down with you."

"No, that's all right. I can find my way."

I walked down to the barn and went inside. Sarah was in the same stall where previously I'd seen Cheryl. Like Cheryl, she was currycombing a horse, a red stallion that looked at me with wide animal eyes and snorted. Sarah glanced at me and put away her currycombs.

I recognized the stallion as the one I'd seen tied to the fence a few days earlier. I crossed my arms and turned on the tape recorder. "Nice horse," I said, not getting too close.

"Not too nice," she said. "But he's fine once you show him who's boss. He doesn't give me any trouble."

I was sure he didn't.

"Does he always lay his ears back and stamp his feet like that when he sees strangers?" I asked.

She slipped out of the stall and shut the gate behind her before the stallion could follow. "Only when they're men," she said. "He doesn't like men."

"I understand that you don't either," I said.

"What's to like?" Her voice was without emotion. She cared nothing about the issue. She didn't care about me, either.

"I wondered if you trained him to feel the way you do. Is that possible?"

Her eyes were fearless. "It could probably be done."

"How would you do it? Dress in men's clothing and beat him from the time he was a colt? Then change clothes and

303

succor him as a woman?"

"That might work. And you could wear men's cologne when you beat him and women's perfume when you healed him and cared for him. Or you might just hire some low-life man to do the beating. It wouldn't be hard to find one."

Unfortunately, she was probably right about that. Most people wouldn't take such a job, but there were always a few who as children were killers of cats and other small animals and who now were adults who would enjoy brutalizing horses, especially if there was money in it.

The stallion snorted and came up to the gate of the stall, ears back, tossing his beautiful hate-filled head. I retreated until my back was against a timber supporting the barn's loft. My discomfort hurried my first question. Her answer and the ones that followed kept me going with increasing confidence.

"Mrs. Bradford, why didn't you tell your daughter to break off her relationship with Harold Hobbes?"

"I don't know what you're talking about."

"Yes, you do. Ethan told you about them. You drove Cheryl away from every other man in her life, but you never even

304

told her you knew about Harold. What was different about Harold?"

"Ethan lied to you. Men lie like rugs. It's their nature."

"I don't think so. He was trying to get into your good graces. He wants you to love him."

"He's my son. He doesn't need to get into my good graces."

"He thinks he does. He thinks you hate him like you hate other men. You knew about Harold but you didn't tell Cheryl that you knew, and there had to be a reason. The reason was murder. You didn't want your daughter to know you killed her lover."

"You watch too many soap operas."

"Did you know Hobbes had a vasectomy not long before he was killed?"

For the first time she showed some emotion. "The rotten bastard!"

"You can guess why he had the operation, can't you?"

Her mouth became a tight, thin line across her face. She said nothing.

"I think we both know why," I said. "He really was in love with Cheryl. They planned to go away together. But he knew something that she didn't know and that he didn't want her to know: that she was his half sister. He got the vasectomy to guarantee that they'd never have children. If there are no children, the arguments against incest don't mean much except as religious tenets or social conventions. Harold wasn't religious and he flouted social convention." I looked into her furious eyes. "Your daughter didn't know that she and Harold had the same father, but you did. Your philandering husband slept with every woman he could find, including Maud Mayhew."

Her voice was a hiss. "Maud's a slut. Always was. And her brat was worse than his father."

"Ollie Mattes was another of his bastards."

"Yes. Another toad."

"And Ron Pierson was just as bad."

"Worse. He thinks his money makes him better than my family. He's building that château just to rub our faces in it."

I half imagined venom coming from her fangs.

"When some vandal smashed all of the windows in that house, a lot of people were pleased. But you wanted more, so you went there to finish the job. You drove over Norton's Point Beach so the ferryman couldn't testify that you'd ridden the On Time that evening. What did you have in mind for Pierson's house? Fire?"

She leaned against the gate of the stall and studied me with ancient, fearless eyes. "What if I did?"

"Ollie Mattes had just been hired as watchman and he was there when you arrived. You didn't expect him, but you knew each other. He turned his back and you hit him."

"You're imagining things."

"You're the right height and you're strong and you hated both Ollie and Ron Pierson. I think you probably used your baseball bat on Ollie. I saw you hit a softball a long way from the southpaw side of the plate. Whoever killed Ollie was left-handed and about your size. I don't know if you meant to kill him, but I think you must have panicked after you hit him. You rolled his body down the bluff to make it look like an accident, and you left then because you didn't dare hang around long enough to torch the place. You went home the way you'd come."

"I've never driven on the beach in my life."

"The sand under your SUV says different."

"You think you're pretty smart, don't you?"

"No smarter than the cops, just a few minutes ahead of them. They'll be along. You killed Harold Hobbes, too, when you found out about him and your daughter. You drove to his house and beat his head in. Did you break your bat that time, or was it just so bloody that you couldn't get it clean? You had a brand-new one when I saw you play ball."

"They'll never find the old one because I burned it," she said. "You're boring me." But she didn't look bored.

"Ollie's death might have been an accident," I said, "but you made sure of Harold's because you hated him the most of all. You'd hated him before on general principles but now he was having incestuous sex with your simple, innocent daughter, a woman he knew was his half sister. You can argue that you saved her from a totally immoral predator. Your motive might seem noble to the judge and jury who try you. It might get you less than a life sentence."

She looked almost serene. "I won't be serving any sentence at all, Mr. Jackson. Do you know why? Because I'm dying. That's also why you can't threaten me in any way. In the eyes of the law I may be a murderer, but when you're already dying you're beyond the law and you can do things other people wouldn't dare do. It makes you free." She smiled icily. "It lets you kill people who deserve it, for instance. My daughter is safe now and she'll never know that she was seduced by her own worthless brother."

"Your killing days are over now," I said.

Her thin lips curled. "I don't know how much intelligence it took for you to find me out, but it couldn't have taken much because men are not very bright, so I imagine that others will soon be coming along to arrest me. They too will fail to frighten me."

"They may not frighten you, but they can put you in jail for the last days of your life."

She smiled a skeletal smile. "Perhaps, but you won't be there to see it happen." And so saying she threw open the gate of the stall and the great red stallion made a feral sound and rushed at me, all teeth and flying hooves.

I didn't have time to think or to panic. I ducked behind the post I was leaning on, and the furious horse, mane flying, smashed into it, bounced to one side, and came around after me, neck stretched out, teeth and front hooves reaching for me.

Sarah Bradford filled my eyes. She stood like a statue beside the open gate of the stall. I plunged across the space between us and grabbed at her arm to pull her into the stall, where we'd be safe. But she jerked away, so I went in by myself and slammed the gate shut behind me.

The stallion was a burst of lightning, his flashing hooves were thunder, his eyes were mad. He crashed into the gate but it held; he reared and smashed at it with his hooves. I backed to the far wall.

Frustrated, the horse danced away and Sarah, smiling like a wolf, said, "I'll just unlock this gate for him." She turned toward the gate and reached for the latch, but as she did so the stallion screamed and rushed forward once again. It reared and slashed at the gate with those great hooves and struck Sarah. She fell and the stallion, wild-eyed, pounded her and then pounded what had once been her until, at last, it snorted and sidestepped away, its ears flat, its forelegs covered with blood.

There was a door leading from the stall out into the corral, and I went out that way and up to the house to call the Chilmark police.

27

Two weeks later Zee and I were lying side by side on the old bedspread that serves as our beach blanket while the kids were making casts with their little rods. They were not having any more luck than Zee and I had had. If there were any fish out there, they didn't care for the bait we were offering them.

We were on East Beach, about halfway between the Jetties and the point of Cape Pogue, and up and down the beach on either side of us were other SUVs and people on beach blankets and in the water, and fishermen also failing to catch fish. Some people, like me, were enjoying a postluncheon beer.

Overhead, the early afternoon sun was hot in a sky half filled with clouds drifting to the east, and while our offspring patiently cast, reeled in, and cast again, Zee and I worked on our tans. Later, in the privacy of our front yard, we would tan the parts now covered with the small patches of cloth that were officially our bathing suits.

"So there won't be any trials?" asked Zee.

"None that I know of," I said. "I don't plan to rat on the Silencer as long as he stays out of business, and Sarah Bradford is in her posttrial stage. Unless, that is, the Christians and others are right about there being a god of justice in the hereafter, in which case she might be looking for a heavenly lawyer as she heads for the celestial dock."

"It must be frustrating for the police not to have anybody to arrest for the two murders."

"They have my tape, so they have Sarah's confession, such as it is. I don't think they'll spend much more time on the case. They have other things to do."

"Such as?"

"The usual. A summer of being patient with tourists who want to know how to find the bridge to Falmouth."

"Ah, yes. The famous bridge to Falmouth."

"Some people don't believe that there isn't one. They insist they got here by driving over it."

"What do the cops do when they meet one of them?"

"They tell them to take the road to Vineyard Haven, and the people drive off feeling good about winning the argument."

"What happens when they get to Vineyard Haven and there isn't any bridge?"

"An unsolved mystery. The cops never see them again. The other day a guy stopped beside Tony D'Agostine and asked, 'Is this the right road?' Tony smiled and assured him that it certainly was and the guy drove off happy."

"Did anybody say which road to where?"

"The guy didn't say and Tony didn't ask."

"Do the cops do anything not having to do with sending tourists on wild-goose chases?"

"Sure. For instance, right now they're trying to prove that one of the guys who's running for county commissioner and is a favorite to win is also the island's biggest drug dealer. They can't prove he's a dealer so they can't even hint that he is. But he is."

"Why can't they get him?"

"Because he only sells to four people and they sell to everybody else. None of the four people will squeal so the cops

313

can't lay a hand on him."

"How do they know it's him, then?"

"Because the four people have said so. It's just that they've never said so on tape. They think it's pretty funny. They won't testify against him and why should they, since he's their meal ticket? And even if they get busted they just lie under oath and they're out of jail almost before they go in. It's harder than it should be to make a righteous bust on Martha's Vineyard, but the cops keep at it."

"We live in a wonderful world. Tell me more about Sarah Bradford catching your eye."

"It was all small stuff. She was a real man-hater, she was the right size, she was left-handed and strong and knew how to swing a bat. She knew Harold was another of her husband's bastards, and when Ethan told her about Harold and Cheryl, she never told Cheryl she knew, which was completely out of character, since normally she worked hard at running off Cheryl's men. She lied about never driving on the beach. It all added up. Both times, once after the weekly softball game, she drove to and from Chappy over Norton's Point Beach, but the biologist never saw her because the biologist left at five."

"Do you really think that she may have killed George Pease, too? Her own son-in-law?"

"I think it could be. Pease was killed by a horse he was trying to train, right there in the Bradford barn where that stallion tried to do me in. It was one of Sarah's horses, and knowing what I know now about Sarah, I wouldn't be surprised if she was down there in the barn the same time her son-in-law was. I imagine she hated Pease just like she hated other men. I know she owned killer horses, and that murder didn't bother her a whit. I can't prove she actually killed anyone, of course."

"God will know."

"I'll look forward to her report."

"What do you think will happen to Cheryl?"

"She's pretty and, unlike you, she's a rich girl. Her biggest problem will be fending off leeches. Maybe her brother will help her filter out the worst of the suitors. She has a good heart, but I don't think she's long on brains, so she needs a little looking after."

"Maybe you should volunteer. You have a fondness for blonde bimbos."

I glanced at her. She had an innocent smile on her face. "No thanks," I said. "I have enough simpleminded women on my hands already."

She grinned. "Touché. I walked right into that one. That'll teach me to be a smart-ass."

"I doubt it."

Above us, surrounded by clouds, there was a blue patch of cloud-eating sky. When clouds blew into it they grew smaller and smaller until they disappeared. Another mystery of the universe. There were many such.

"What about the other players in this drama you've been reviewing?"

"I wasn't reviewing it, I was part of the cast. Sort of, at least. Well, let's see. Ethan may make a deal with cousin Ron Pierson and sell him back the HPM weapon he's perfected. Money makes for strange bedfellows, after all."

"Maybe if they can make a deal it'll heal the war between the Pierson factions. The Hatfields and the McCoys made up, after all, and if they could do it the Piersons can."

"Maybe. Let's see now . . . Helga Mattes and John Lupien can get hitched and live happily ever after. Who's left?"

"How about all of those women Harold Hobbes seduced?"

"I've never thought that seduction between adults was a one-way street," I said. "I think all of the ladies will survive quite well. Maybe Maria Danawa and Paul Fox can have a double wedding with Helga and John. What do you think?"

"I feel bad about Maud Mayhew. She got nothing but grief out of this."

"Her son wasn't much of a loss."

"You can say that, but he was her son, and he finally actually loved someone, even though it was his own half sister."

"I wonder if he knew what love is."

"He loved her enough to have that vasectomy."

"There was that."

"And he was going to take her away where no one would know them and they could start a new life."

"Yes."

"I feel bad about Maud."

"She's a tough old bird. She's outlasted three husbands and she can probably survive this. The question is whether she can survive Ron Pierson and people like him building castles on Chappaquiddick."

"Maybe the battle to make Chappy a gated community will rouse her élan vital."

"Could be."

We looked up at the spot of cloud-eating

sky. It was still there. I could hear the sound of laughter from somewhere down the beach.

I rolled over until I was lying across Zee's sun-warmed body, and put an elbow on the bedspread on either side of her head. She looked up at me with her wide, dark eyes.

"Aha, me proud beauty," I said with a leer. "You are in my power at last."

She fluttered her long lashes. "Oh, dastardly villain, you would not dare to treat me so if Lord Studley or brother Jack were here."

"Your precious Studley is with his regiment fighting fuzzy-wuzzies and your dear brother Jack is far at sea and cannot save you this time."

She put her bronze arms around me. "Help, help," she whispered.

"Your cries are in vain," I said, giving her a kiss. "Surrender."

"Never, vile scoundrel."

"Then I shall wreak my wicked will upon you."

"You may possess my body, beast, but you will never possess my soul."

"Pa! Ma! Look! Look!" Joshua's voice was filled with excitement.

We looked and saw little Diana down by

the surf, her tiny rod bent nearly in two.

"She's got a fish!" shouted her brother.

We were on our feet in an instant and beside our daughter a moment later.

"Reel down like we showed you," said Zee. "Then raise the rod and reel down again. You can back up, too."

Diana did both and after a battle, a fish came flopping up onto the sand.

"It's a keeper," I said. "Good work! We can have him for supper."

Diana was beaming and panting. "He almost pulled me in. I thought he was a big shark."

"It's better than a shark," said Zee, hugging her. "It's a flounder, and it's your very first fish. We're proud of you!" She smiled at me. "I didn't notice you rigging her up for flounder."

"There are no blues around so I figured she couldn't lose by trying for these guys."

On both sides of us the fishermen were staring, wondering what sort of fish Diana had caught or perhaps using the flounder as an excuse to look at Zee in her bikini. Both reasons were understandable.

I took the fish off Diana's hook and put it in the fish box. Then I rebaited the hook and sent my daughter back down to the water.

Five minutes later Zee and I had our light rods rigged with sinkers and baited hooks and had joined our children and the other fishermen in having a go at flounder. It was a beautiful Vineyard day and I was happy.

"Pa."

"What, Diana?"

Her smile and eyes were bright. "This is even funner than the computer!"

Such a wise child. Took after her father. No doubt about it.

Recipes

Chicken and Snow Peas

(Serves 3–4)

This is a simple, one-dish meal. If you don't like chicken, you can use shrimp or scallops instead. If you like it hotter, add hot sauce or red pepper to taste.

J.W. cooks this dish in the book.

2 tsps. soy sauce
2 tsps. cornstarch
2 tsps. sherry
2 tsps. water
¼ tsp. white pepper
4 tbsps. cooking oil
1½ lbs. chicken breasts, boned, skinned, and cut into bite-sized sections
1 clove minced garlic
8 ozs. sliced mushrooms

½ c. sliced bamboo shoots
¼ lb. snow peas (Chinese pea pods)

Sauce

½ c. water
1 tbsp. sherry
2 tbsps. soy sauce
½ tsp. sugar
1 tsp. cooking oil
1 tbsp. cornstarch

Mix sauce and set aside.

Marinate chicken in mixture of soy sauce, cornstarch, sherry, water, pepper, and oil.

Put wok or skillet over high heat. When it's hot, add 1 tablespoon oil. When oil is hot, stir in garlic and half of chicken mixture. Cook about 3 minutes, until chicken centers are no longer pink. Remove chicken and repeat process with remaining chicken.

Remove chicken, add remaining oil. When hot, stir in mushrooms and bamboo shoots for one minute, then add pea pods. After stirring for 3 minutes, return chicken to wok. Add sauce and stir until sauce is boiling and has thickened.

Serve with rice.

Spaghetti Sauce

(Serves 8)

Like most recipes, this one can be modified according to your taste. J.W. likes it just the way it is.

1 large onion, chopped
2 cloves (at least) garlic, minced
½ c. cooking oil
1 sweet red or green pepper, chopped
8 ozs. sliced mushrooms
1 lb. ground beef (or chicken, if you
    don't eat mammals)
1 lb. hot Italian sausage, cut into
    bite-sized pieces
½–1 c. red wine
1 can cream of mushroom soup
    (the secret ingredient)
1 6-oz. can tomato paste
1 tbsp. dried parsley
1 tbsp. each dried sage, rosemary,
    thyme
1 tbsp. Dona Flora's "Bean Supreme"
    (a wonderful combination of herbs
    and spices available from Dona Flora,
    PO Box 77, La Conner, WA 98257)
Salt and pepper to taste
Ground Parmesan cheese to taste

In a large frying pan over medium heat, sauté onion and garlic in a bit of oil; remove from pan, add more oil if necessary, and sauté pepper and mushrooms; remove from pan, add remaining oil, and brown ground meat and sausage.

Return veggies to pan, add wine, and stir in remaining ingredients. Cook, covered, over low heat for 20 minutes, stirring occasionally.

Serve over pasta and top with ground Parmesan cheese. Delish!

Seviche

This excellent cold dish consists of fish "cooked" only by a lime marinade. The best fish to use when making seviche are oily ones such as bluefish because the marinating process eliminates the oil. Since Martha's Vineyard waters contain a lot of bluefish, that is the species J.W. uses.

2 c. of fish fillets cut into ½-inch cubes
2 small hot green peppers, finely chopped
1 large tomato, peeled and chopped
½ c. onion, chopped

1/4 c. red pepper, finely chopped
2 cloves garlic, minced
1/2 c. tomato juice
1/3 c. lime juice
1/3 c. olive oil
1 tbsp. parsley, finely chopped
1/2 tbsp. coriander (cilantro), finely
   chopped
2 sprigs thyme, finely chopped
Salt and pepper to taste

Combine all ingredients and let them stand in the refrigerator overnight. Seviche is best served ice-cold.

About the Author

Philip R. Craig grew up on a small cattle ranch southeast of Durango, Colorado. He earned his MFA at the University of Iowa Writers' Workshop and was for many years a professor of literature at Wheelock College in Boston. He and his wife live on Martha's Vineyard.

We hope you have enjoyed this Large Print book. Other Thorndike, Wheeler or Chivers Press Large Print books are available at your library or directly from the publishers.

For more information about current and upcoming titles, please call or write, without obligation, to:

Publisher
Thorndike Press
295 Kennedy Memorial Drive
Waterville, ME 04901
Tel. (800) 223-1244

Or visit our Web site at:
www.gale.com/thorndike
www.gale.com/wheeler

OR

Chivers Large Print
published by BBC Audiobooks Ltd
St James House, The Square
Lower Bristol Road
Bath BA2 3SB
England
Tel. +44(0) 800 136919
email: bbcaudiobooks@bbc.co.uk
www.bbcaudiobooks.co.uk

All our Large Print titles are designed for easy reading, and all our books are made to last.